PAPERCUTZ SLICES

# Harry Potty and the Deathly Boring

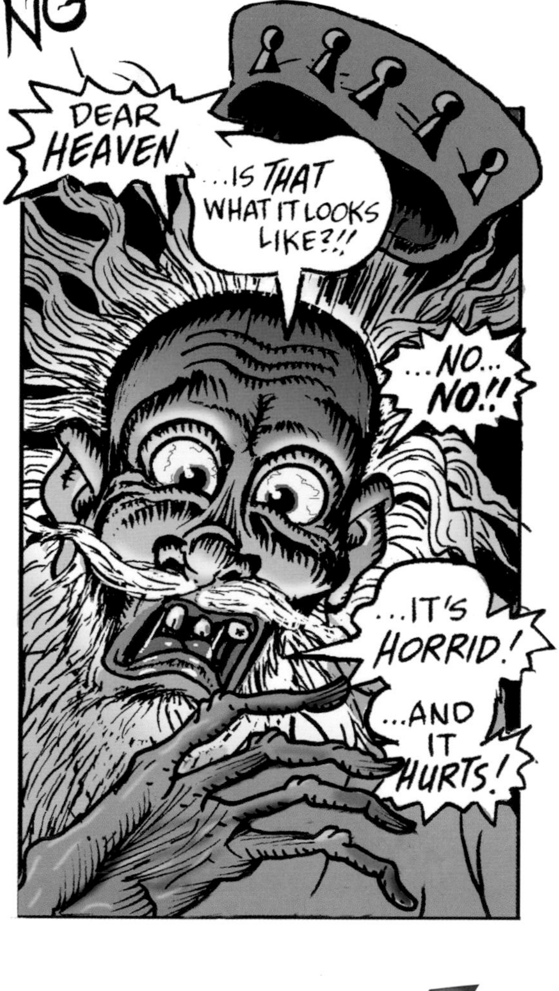
DEAR HEAVEN
...IS THAT WHAT IT LOOKS LIKE?!!
...NO... NO!!
...IT'S HORRID!
...AND IT HURTS!

PAPERCUTZ

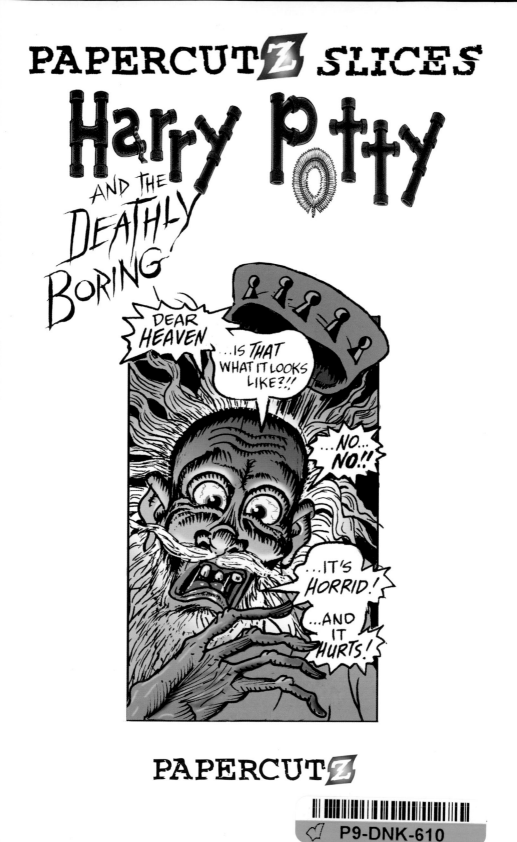

# PAPERCUTZ SLICES

## Graphic Novels Available from PAPERCUTZ (Who else..?!)

Graphic Novel #1
"Harry Potty and
the Deathly Boring"

Graphic Novel #2
"breaking down"

Graphic Novel #3
"Percy Jerkson & The
Ovolactovegetarians"

Graphic Novel #4
"The Hunger Pains"

## NEW! PAPERCUTZ SLICES is now available from COMIXOLOGY
### Now you can read PAPERCUTZ SLICES and look like you're conducting serious business!

PAPERCUTZ SLICES graphic novels are available at booksellers everywhere. At bookstores, comicbook stores, online, out of the trunk in the back of Rick Parker's car, and who knows where else? If you still are unable to find PAPERCUTZ SLICES (probably because it sold out) you can always order directly from Papercutz—but it'll cost you! PAPERCUTZ SLICES is available in paperback for $6.99 each; in hardcover for $10.99 each. But that's not the worst part-- please add $4.00 for postage and handling for the first book, and add $1.00 for each additional book. Going to your favorite bookseller, buying online, or even getting a copy from your local library doesn't seem so bad now, does it? But if you still insist on ordering from Papercutz, and just to make everything just a little bit more complicated, please make your check payable to NBM Publishing. Don't ask why—it's just how it works. Send to: Papercutz, 160 Broadway, Ste. 700, East Wing, New York, NY 10038
Or call 800 886 1223 (9-6 EST M-F) MC-Visa-Amex accepted

### www.papercutz.com

# PAPERCUTZ SLICES

# Harry Potty
## AND THE DEATHLY BORING

STEFAN PETRUCHA
Writer
RICK PARKER
Artist

New York

"Harry Potty and the Deathly Boring"

STEFAN PETRUCHA – Writer
RICK PARKER – Artist

TROY HAHN
Production

MICHAEL PETRANEK
Associate Editor

JIM SALICRUP
Editor-in-Chief

ISBN: 978-1-59707-217-5 paperback edition
ISBN: 978-1-59707-218-2 hardcover edition

Copyright © 2010 by Stefan Petrucha and Barking Dog Studios. All rights reserved.

Printed in China
May 2012 by New Era Printing LTD
Trend Centre, 29-31 Cheung Lee St.
Rm. 1101-1103, 11/F, Chaiwan

Distributed by Macmillan.

Second Printing

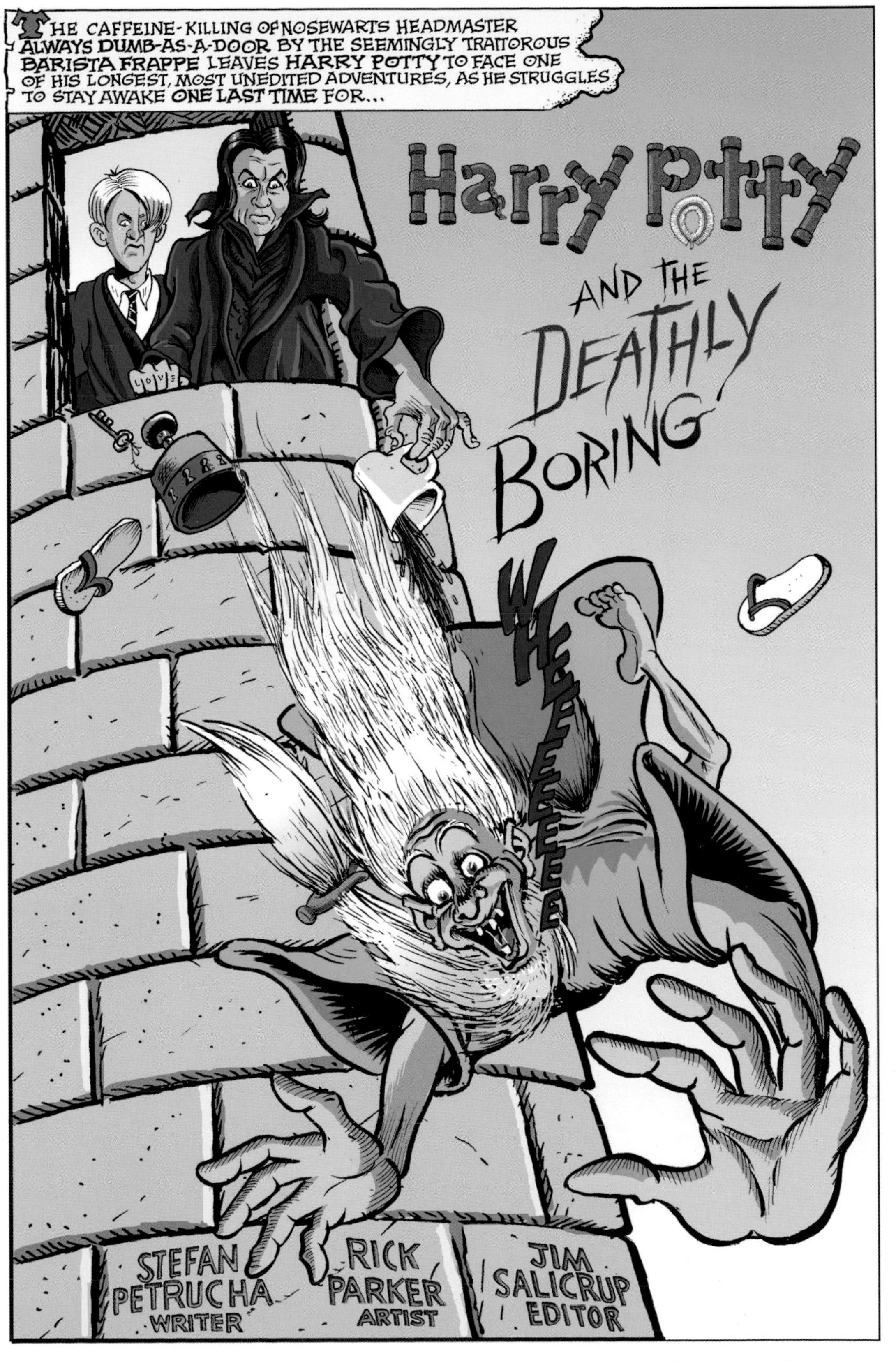
THE CAFFEINE-KILLING OF NOSEWARTS HEADMASTER ALWAYS DUMB-AS-A-DOOR BY THE SEEMINGLY TRAITOROUS BARISTA FRAPPE LEAVES HARRY POTTY TO FACE ONE OF HIS LONGEST, MOST UNEDITED ADVENTURES, AS HE STRUGGLES TO STAY AWAKE ONE LAST TIME FOR...
Harry Potty
AND THE DEATHLY BORING
LOVE
WHEEEEEEEEE
STEFAN PETRUCHA WRITER
RICK PARKER ARTIST
JIM SALICRUP EDITOR

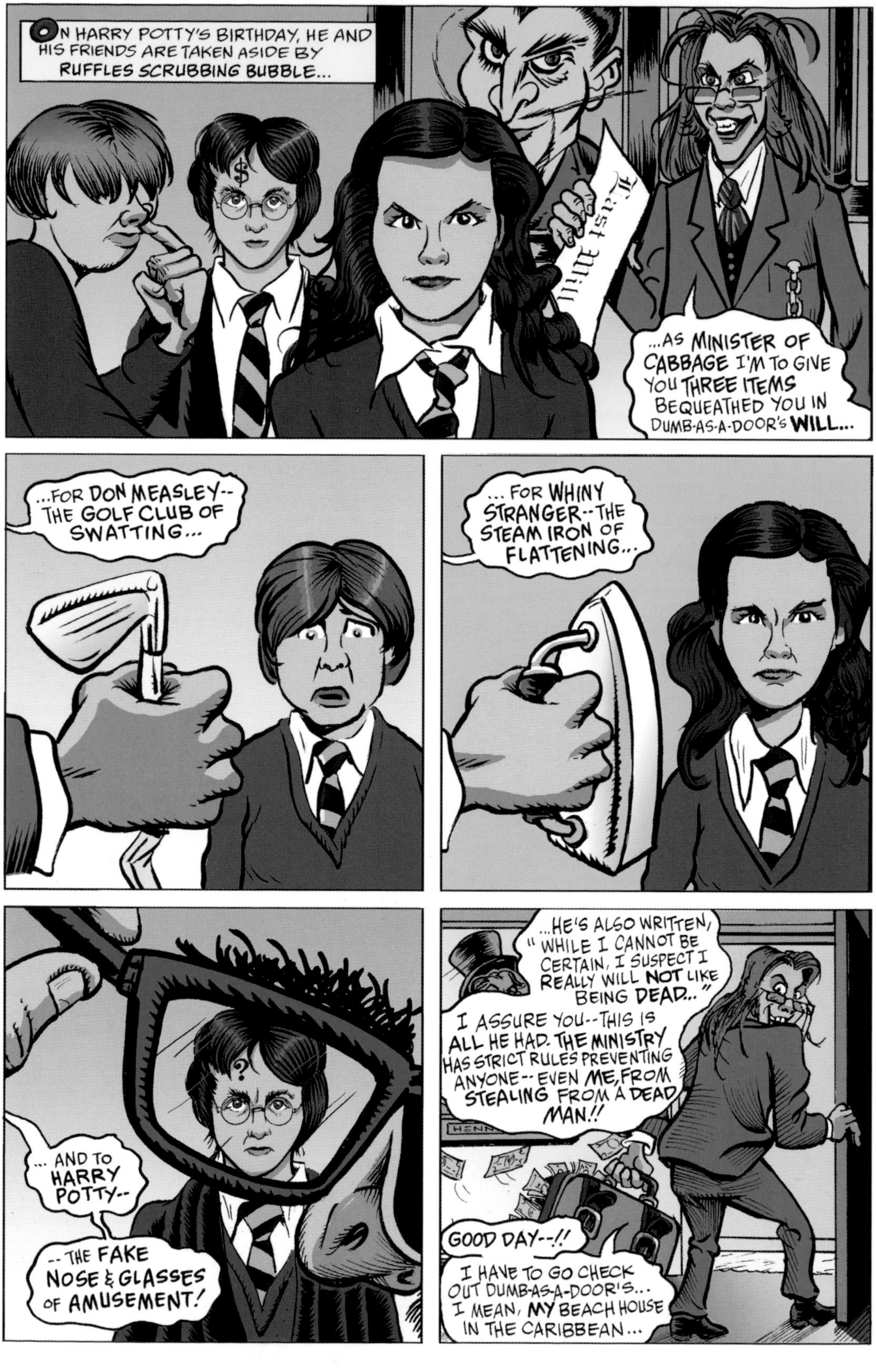
ON HARRY POTTY'S BIRTHDAY, HE AND HIS FRIENDS ARE TAKEN ASIDE BY RUFFLES SCRUBBING BUBBLE...
...AS MINISTER OF CABBAGE I'M TO GIVE YOU THREE ITEMS BEQUEATHED YOU IN DUMB-AS-A-DOOR'S WILL...
...FOR DON MEASLEY-- THE GOLF CLUB OF SWATTING...
... FOR WHINY STRANGER-- THE STEAM IRON OF FLATTENING...
... AND TO HARRY POTTY--
-- THE FAKE NOSE & GLASSES OF AMUSEMENT!
...HE'S ALSO WRITTEN, "WHILE I CANNOT BE CERTAIN, I SUSPECT I REALLY WILL NOT LIKE BEING DEAD..."
I ASSURE YOU--THIS IS ALL HE HAD. THE MINISTRY HAS STRICT RULES PREVENTING ANYONE-- EVEN ME, FROM STEALING FROM A DEAD MAN!!
GOOD DAY--!!
I HAVE TO GO CHECK OUT DUMB-AS-A-DOOR'S... I MEAN, MY BEACH HOUSE IN THE CARIBBEAN...

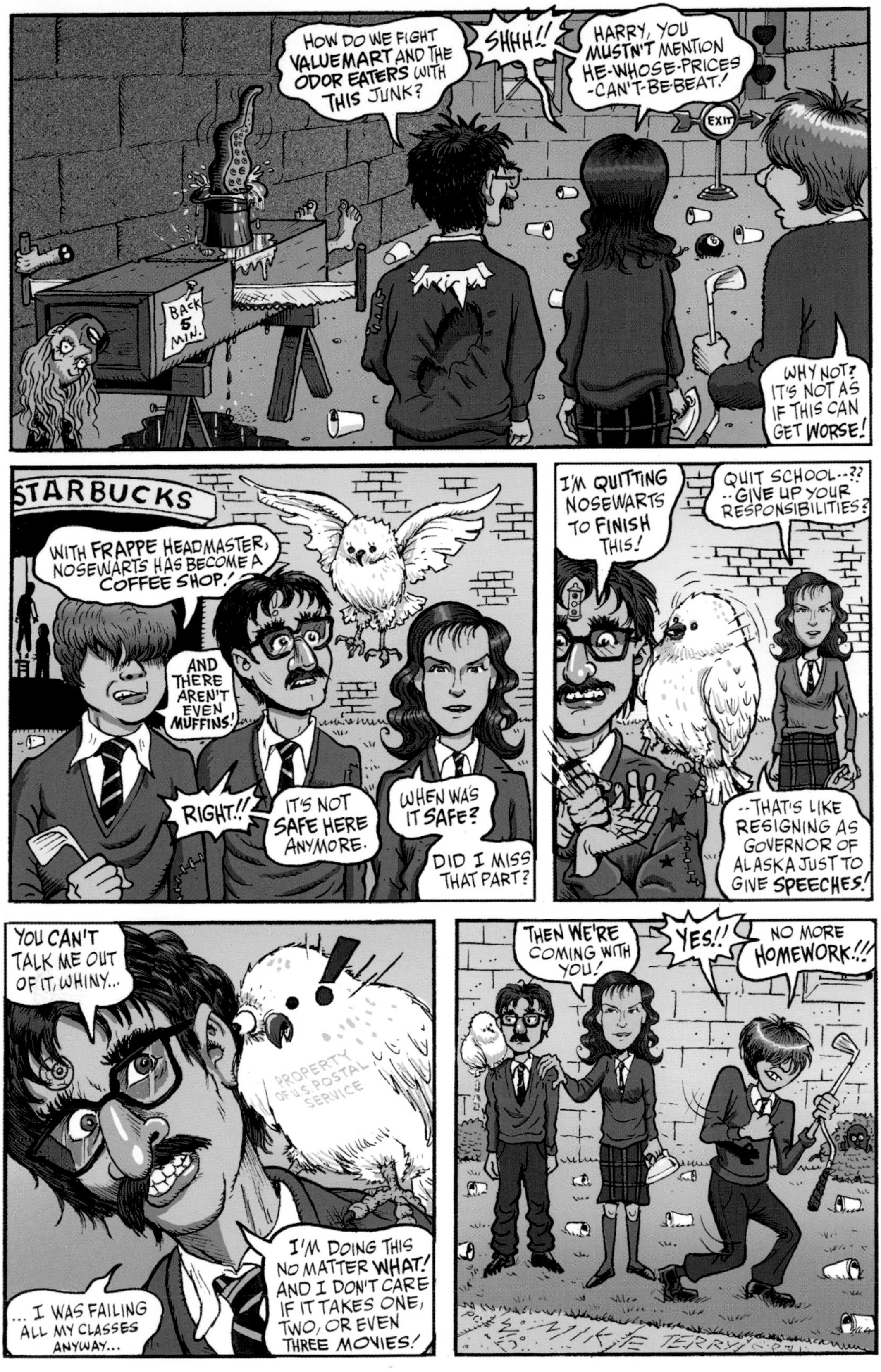
HOW DO WE FIGHT VALUEMART AND THE ODOR EATERS WITH THIS JUNK?
SHHH!!
HARRY, YOU MUSTN'T MENTION HE-WHOSE-PRICES-CAN'T-BE-BEAT!
EXIT
BACK 5 MIN.
WHY NOT? IT'S NOT AS IF THIS CAN GET WORSE!
STARBUCKS
WITH FRAPPE HEADMASTER, NOSEWARTS HAS BECOME A COFFEE SHOP!
AND THERE AREN'T EVEN MUFFINS!
RIGHT!!
IT'S NOT SAFE HERE ANYMORE.
WHEN WAS IT SAFE?
DID I MISS THAT PART?
I'M QUITTING NOSEWARTS TO FINISH THIS!
QUIT SCHOOL--?? ..GIVE UP YOUR RESPONSIBILITIES?
--THAT'S LIKE RESIGNING AS GOVERNOR OF ALASKA JUST TO GIVE SPEECHES!
YOU CAN'T TALK ME OUT OF IT, WHINY...
!
PROPERTY OF U.S. POSTAL SERVICE
...I WAS FAILING ALL MY CLASSES ANYWAY...
I'M DOING THIS NO MATTER WHAT! AND I DON'T CARE IF IT TAKES ONE, TWO, OR EVEN THREE MOVIES!
THEN WE'RE COMING WITH YOU!
YES!!
NO MORE HOMEWORK!!!

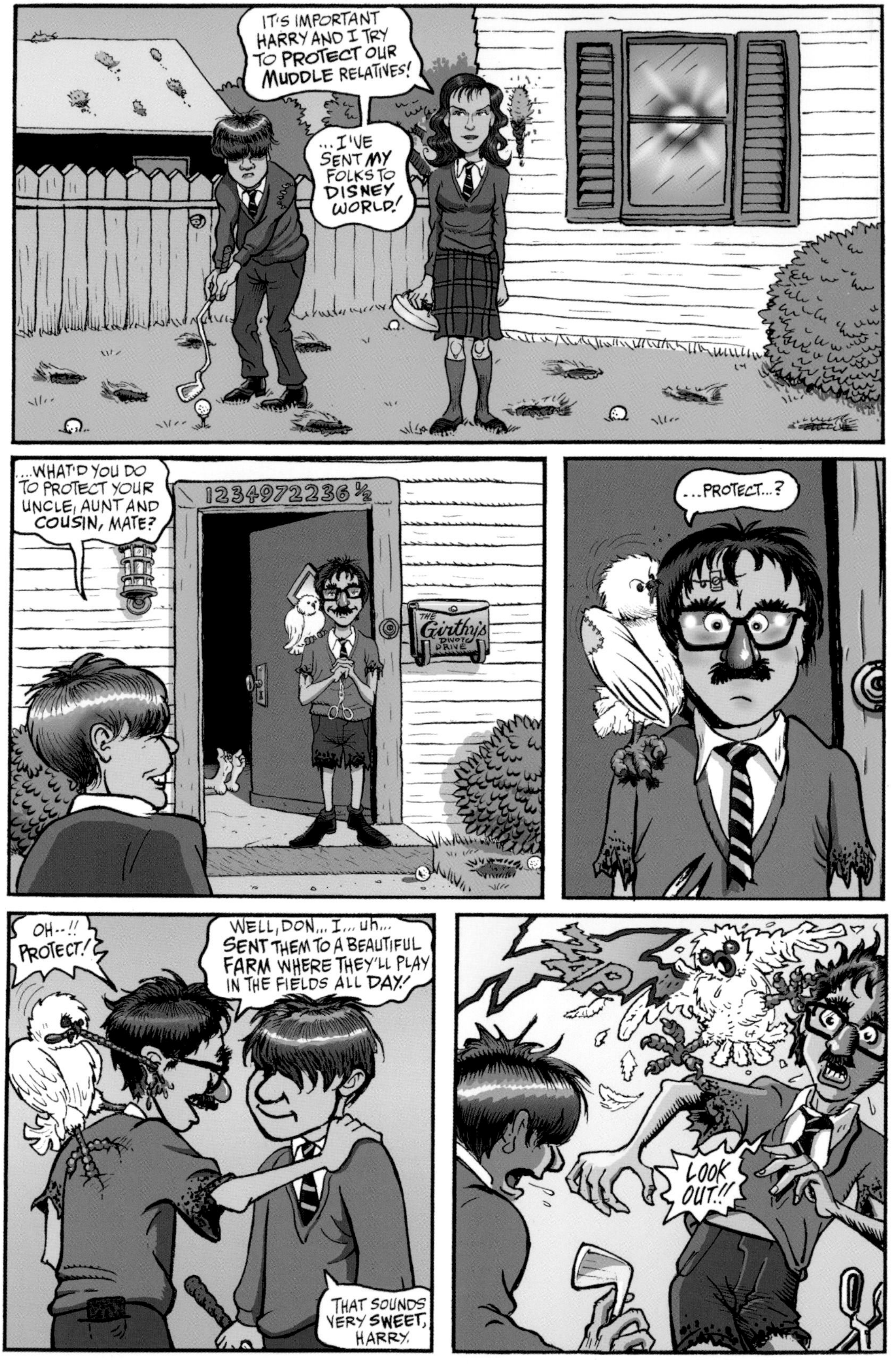
IT'S IMPORTANT HARRY AND I TRY TO PROTECT OUR MUDDLE RELATIVES!
...I'VE SENT MY FOLKS TO DISNEY WORLD!
...WHAT'D YOU DO TO PROTECT YOUR UNCLE, AUNT AND COUSIN, MATE?
1234972236 ½
THE Girthy's DIVOT DRIVE
...PROTECT...?
OH--!! PROTECT!
WELL, DON... I... uh... SENT THEM TO A BEAUTIFUL FARM WHERE THEY'LL PLAY IN THE FIELDS ALL DAY!
THAT SOUNDS VERY SWEET, HARRY.
ZAP
LOOK OUT!!

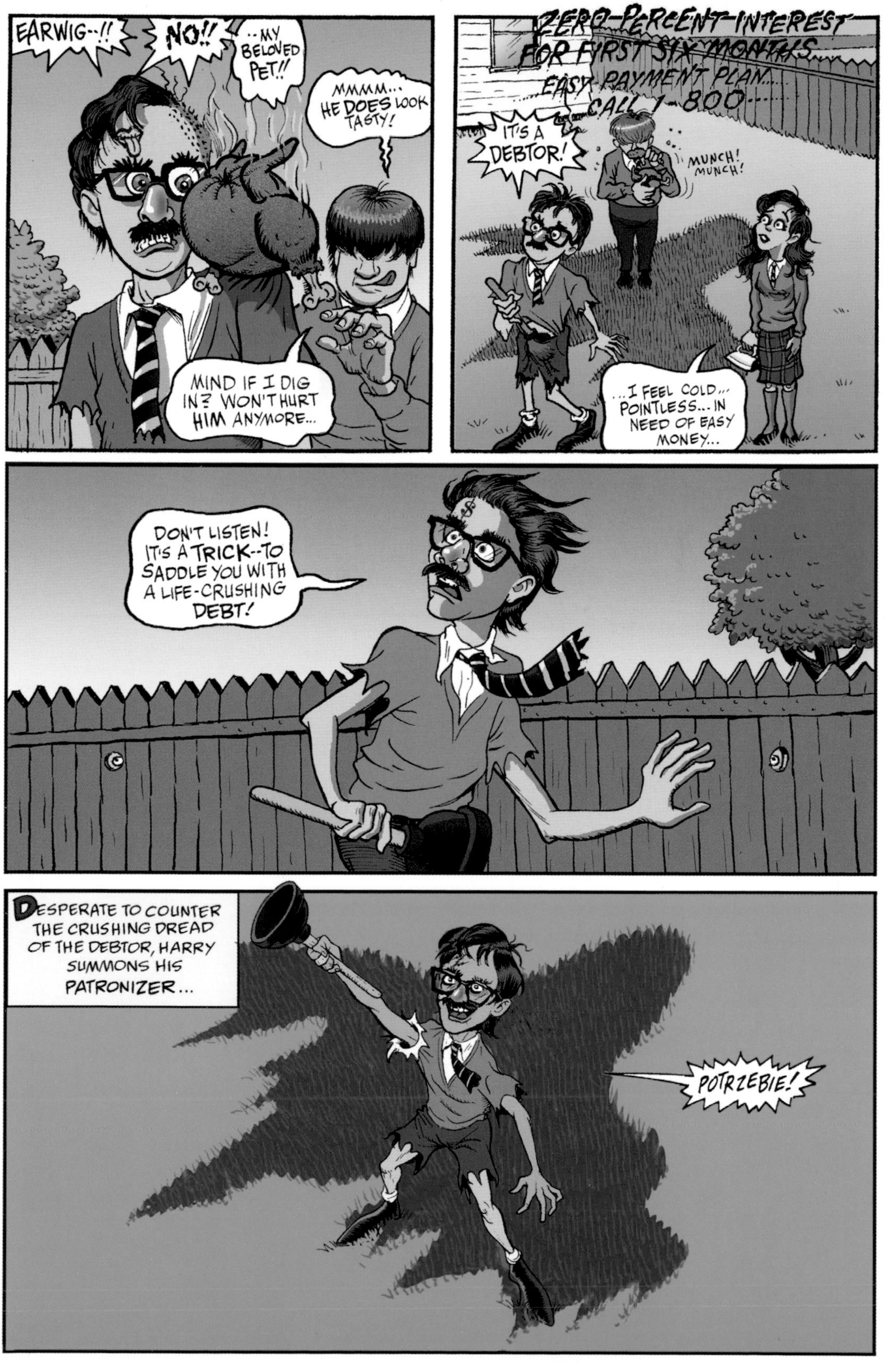
EARWIG--!!
NO!!
..MY BELOVED PET!!
MMMM... HE DOES LOOK TASTY!
MIND IF I DIG IN? WON'T HURT HIM ANYMORE...
ZERO-PERCENT INTEREST FOR FIRST SIX MONTHS... EASY PAYMENT PLAN... CALL 1-800...
IT'S A DEBTOR!
MUNCH! MUNCH!
...I FEEL COLD... POINTLESS... IN NEED OF EASY MONEY...
DON'T LISTEN! IT'S A TRICK--TO SADDLE YOU WITH A LIFE-CRUSHING DEBT!
DESPERATE TO COUNTER THE CRUSHING DREAD OF THE DEBTOR, HARRY SUMMONS HIS PATRONIZER...
POTRZEBIE!

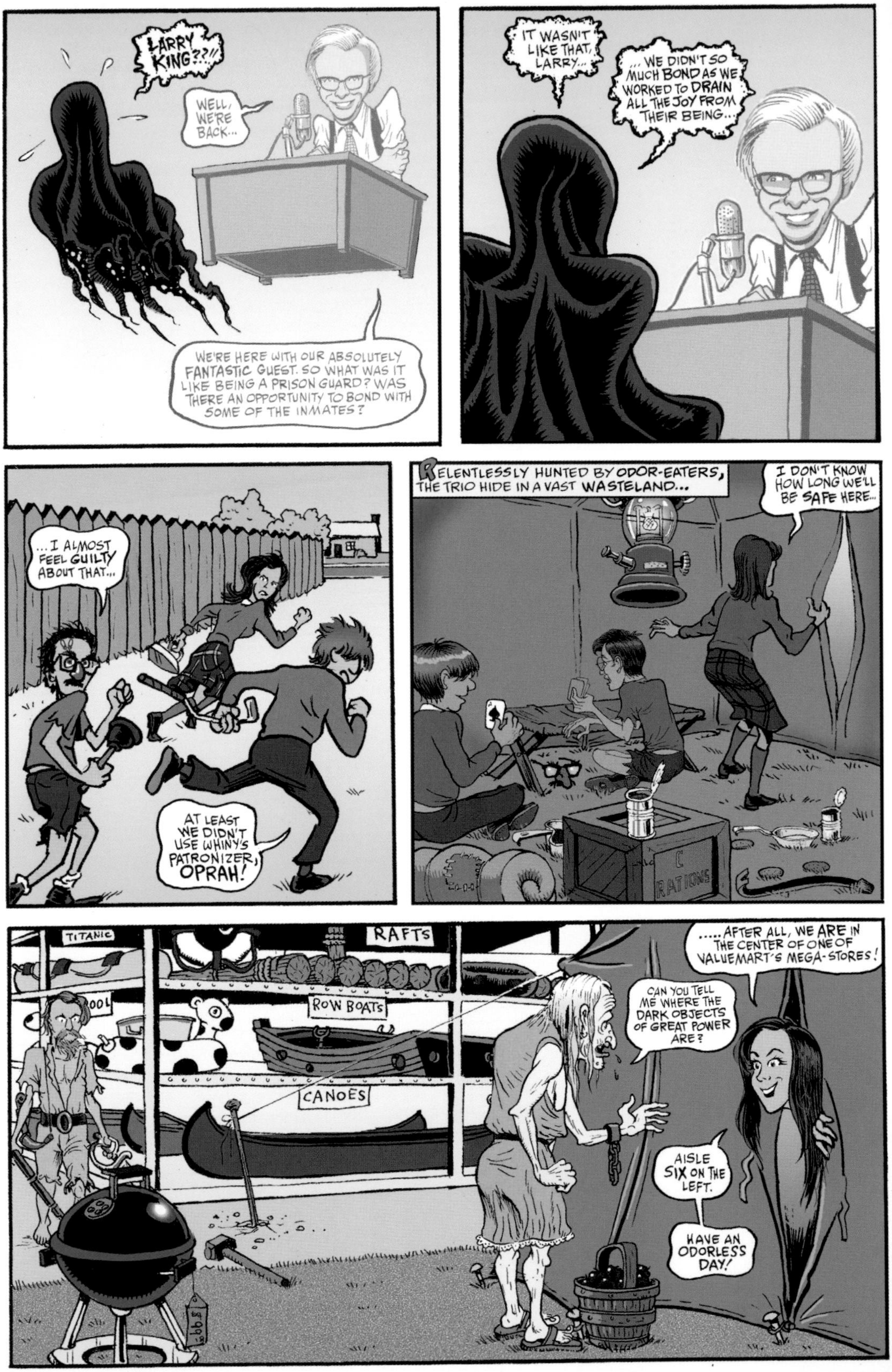
LARRY KING??!!
WELL, WE'RE BACK...
WE'RE HERE WITH OUR ABSOLUTELY FANTASTIC GUEST. SO WHAT WAS IT LIKE BEING A PRISON GUARD? WAS THERE AN OPPORTUNITY TO BOND WITH SOME OF THE INMATES?
IT WASN'T LIKE THAT, LARRY...
...WE DIDN'T SO MUCH BOND AS WE WORKED TO DRAIN ALL THE JOY FROM THEIR BEING...
...I ALMOST FEEL GUILTY ABOUT THAT...
AT LEAST WE DIDN'T USE WHINY'S PATRONIZER, OPRAH!
RELENTLESSLY HUNTED BY ODOR-EATERS, THE TRIO HIDE IN A VAST WASTELAND...
I DON'T KNOW HOW LONG WE'LL BE SAFE HERE...
C RATIONS
TITANIC
RAFTS
ROW BOATS
CANOES
.....AFTER ALL, WE ARE IN THE CENTER OF ONE OF VALUEMART'S MEGA-STORES!
CAN YOU TELL ME WHERE THE DARK OBJECTS OF GREAT POWER ARE?
AISLE SIX ON THE LEFT.
HAVE AN ODORLESS DAY!

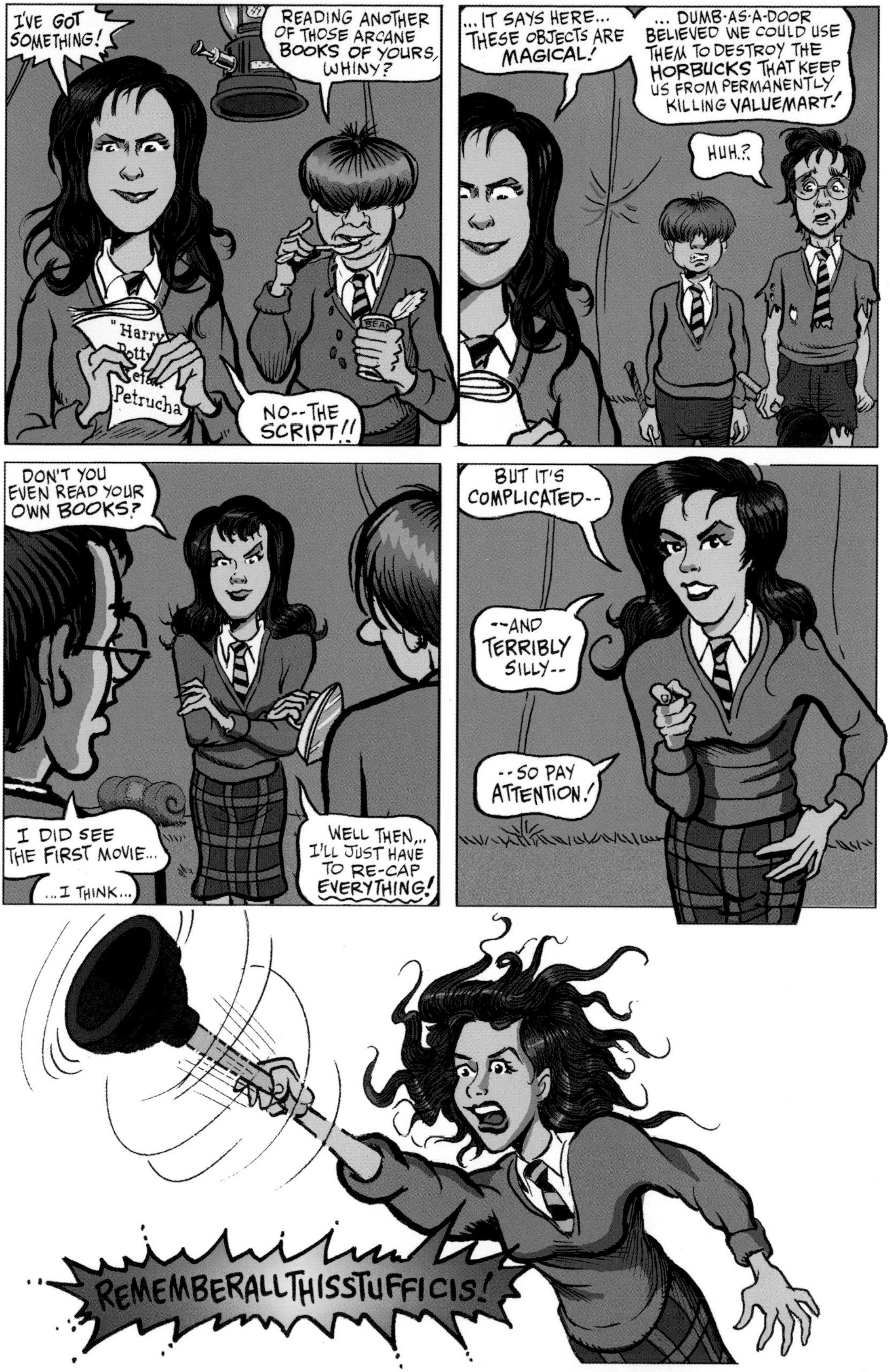
I'VE GOT SOMETHING!
READING ANOTHER OF THOSE ARCANE BOOKS OF YOURS, WHINY?
"Harry Potty" Stefan Petrucha
NO--THE SCRIPT!!
...IT SAYS HERE... THESE OBJECTS ARE MAGICAL!
... DUMB-AS-A-DOOR BELIEVED WE COULD USE THEM TO DESTROY THE HORBUCKS THAT KEEP US FROM PERMANENTLY KILLING VALUEMART!
HUH.?.
DON'T YOU EVEN READ YOUR OWN BOOKS?
I DID SEE THE FIRST MOVIE...
...I THINK...
WELL THEN... I'LL JUST HAVE TO RE-CAP EVERYTHING!
BUT IT'S COMPLICATED--
--AND TERRIBLY SILLY--
--SO PAY ATTENTION!
REMEMBERALLTHISSTUFFICIS!

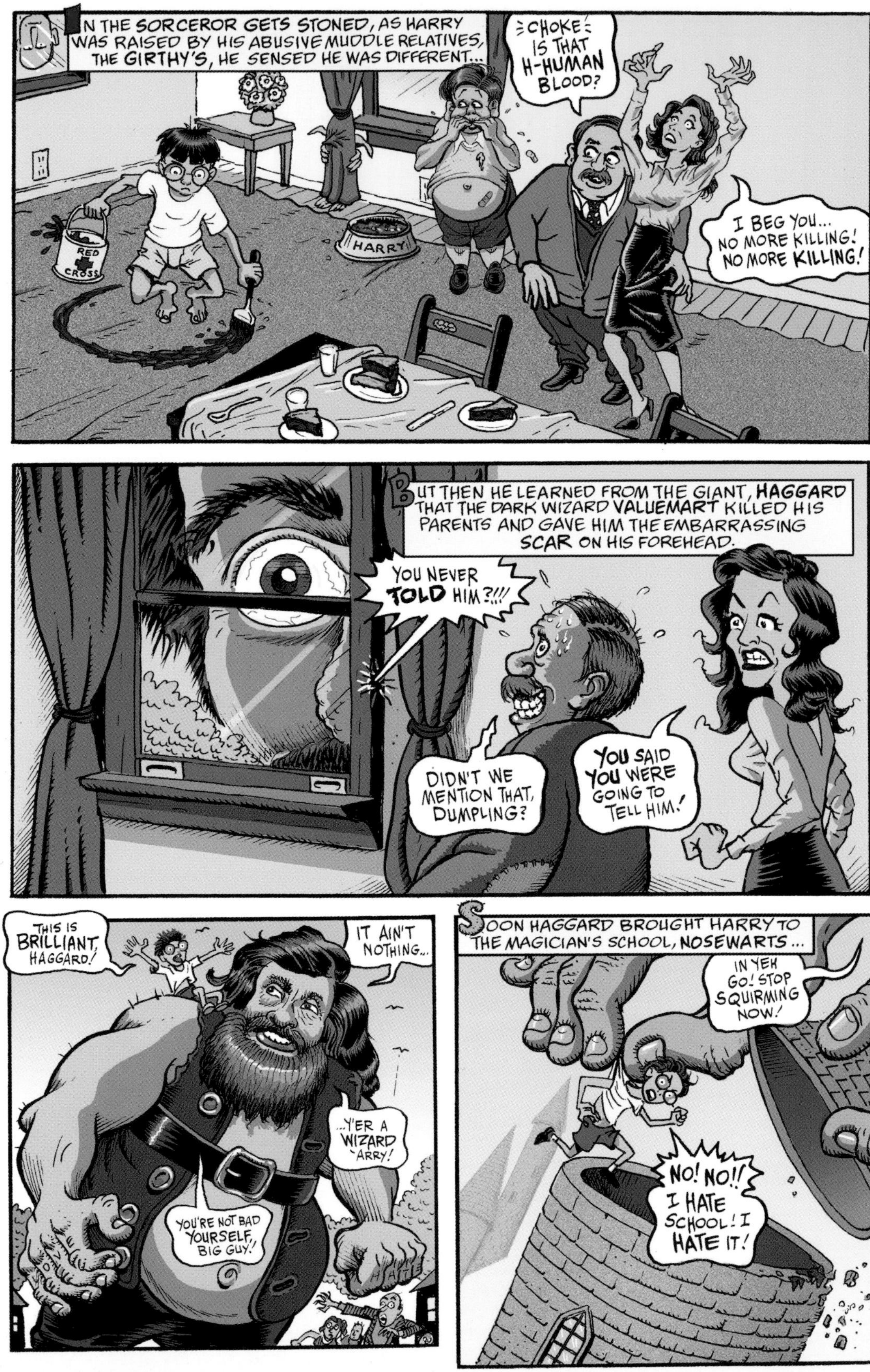
IN THE SORCEROR GETS STONED, AS HARRY WAS RAISED BY HIS ABUSIVE MUDDLE RELATIVES, THE GIRTHY'S, HE SENSED HE WAS DIFFERENT...
CHOKE IS THAT H-HUMAN BLOOD?
RED CROSS
HARRY
I BEG YOU... NO MORE KILLING! NO MORE KILLING!
BUT THEN HE LEARNED FROM THE GIANT, HAGGARD THAT THE DARK WIZARD VALUEMART KILLED HIS PARENTS AND GAVE HIM THE EMBARRASSING SCAR ON HIS FOREHEAD.
YOU NEVER TOLD HIM?!!!
DIDN'T WE MENTION THAT, DUMPLING?
YOU SAID YOU WERE GOING TO TELL HIM!
THIS IS BRILLIANT, HAGGARD!
IT AIN'T NOTHING...
...Y'ER A WIZARD 'ARRY!
YOU'RE NOT BAD YOURSELF, BIG GUY!
SOON HAGGARD BROUGHT HARRY TO THE MAGICIAN'S SCHOOL, NOSEWARTS...
IN YEH GO! STOP SQUIRMING NOW!
NO! NO!! I HATE SCHOOL! I HATE IT!

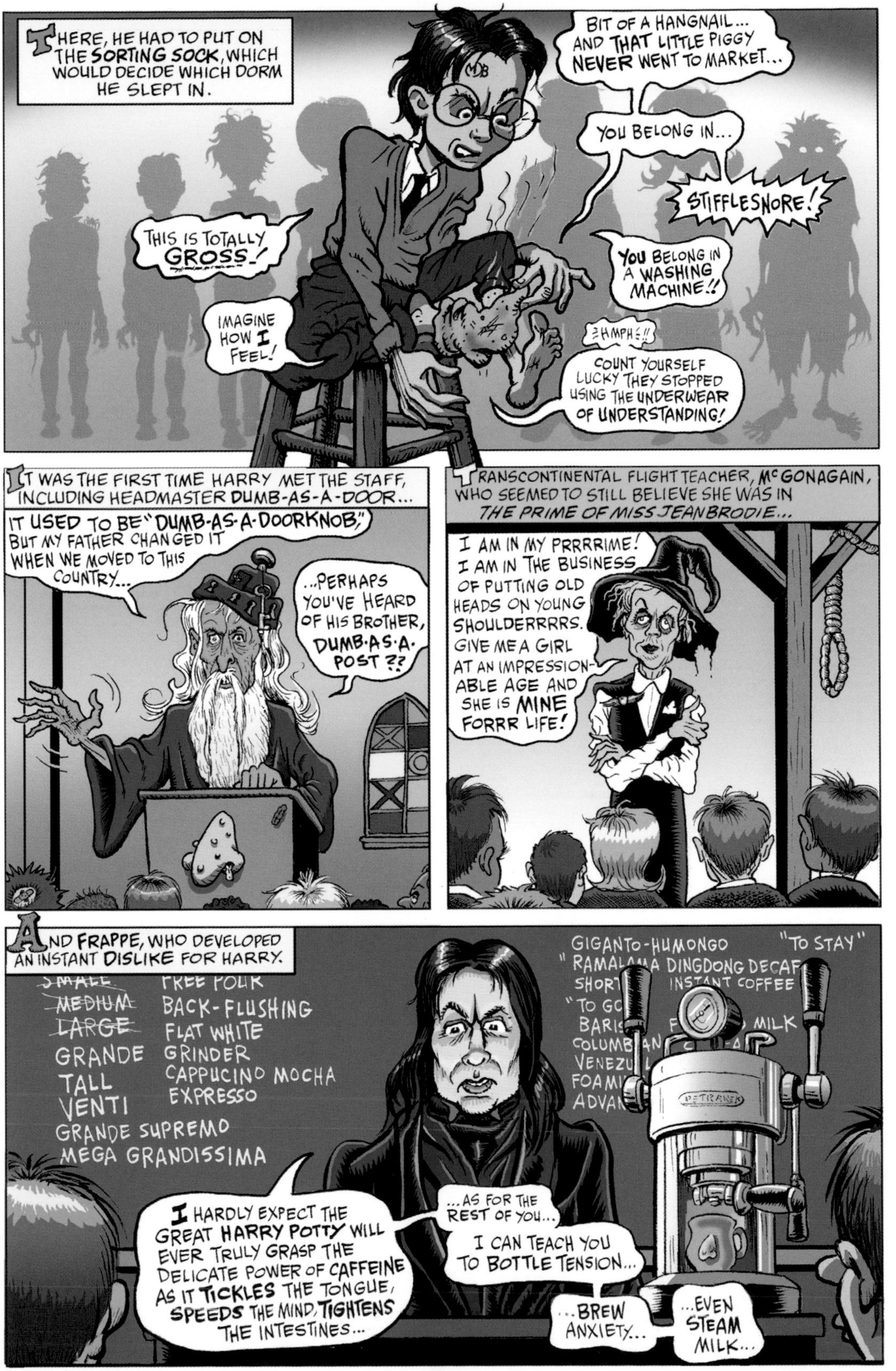
THERE, HE HAD TO PUT ON THE SORTING SOCK, WHICH WOULD DECIDE WHICH DORM HE SLEPT IN.
BIT OF A HANGNAIL... AND THAT LITTLE PIGGY NEVER WENT TO MARKET...
YOU BELONG IN...
STIFFLESNORE!
THIS IS TOTALLY GROSS!
YOU BELONG IN A WASHING MACHINE!!
IMAGINE HOW I FEEL!
HMPH!!
COUNT YOURSELF LUCKY THEY STOPPED USING THE UNDERWEAR OF UNDERSTANDING!
IT WAS THE FIRST TIME HARRY MET THE STAFF, INCLUDING HEADMASTER DUMB-AS-A-DOOR...
IT USED TO BE "DUMB-AS-A-DOORKNOB," BUT MY FATHER CHANGED IT WHEN WE MOVED TO THIS COUNTRY...
...PERHAPS YOU'VE HEARD OF HIS BROTHER, DUMB-AS-A-POST??
TRANSCONTINENTAL FLIGHT TEACHER, McGONAGAIN, WHO SEEMED TO STILL BELIEVE SHE WAS IN THE PRIME OF MISS JEAN BRODIE...
I AM IN MY PRRRRIME! I AM IN THE BUSINESS OF PUTTING OLD HEADS ON YOUNG SHOULDERRRRS. GIVE ME A GIRL AT AN IMPRESSIONABLE AGE AND SHE IS MINE FORRR LIFE!
AND FRAPPE, WHO DEVELOPED AN INSTANT DISLIKE FOR HARRY.
MEDIUM
LARGE
GRANDE
TALL
VENTI
GRANDE SUPREMO
MEGA GRANDISSIMA
FREE POUR
BACK-FLUSHING
FLAT WHITE
GRINDER
CAPPUCINO MOCHA
EXPRESSO
GIGANTO-HUMONGO
"TO STAY"
SHORT
INSTANT COFFEE
I HARDLY EXPECT THE GREAT HARRY POTTY WILL EVER TRULY GRASP THE DELICATE POWER OF CAFFEINE AS IT TICKLES THE TONGUE, SPEEDS THE MIND, TIGHTENS THE INTESTINES...
...AS FOR THE REST OF YOU...
I CAN TEACH YOU TO BOTTLE TENSION...
...BREW ANXIETY...
...EVEN STEAM MILK...

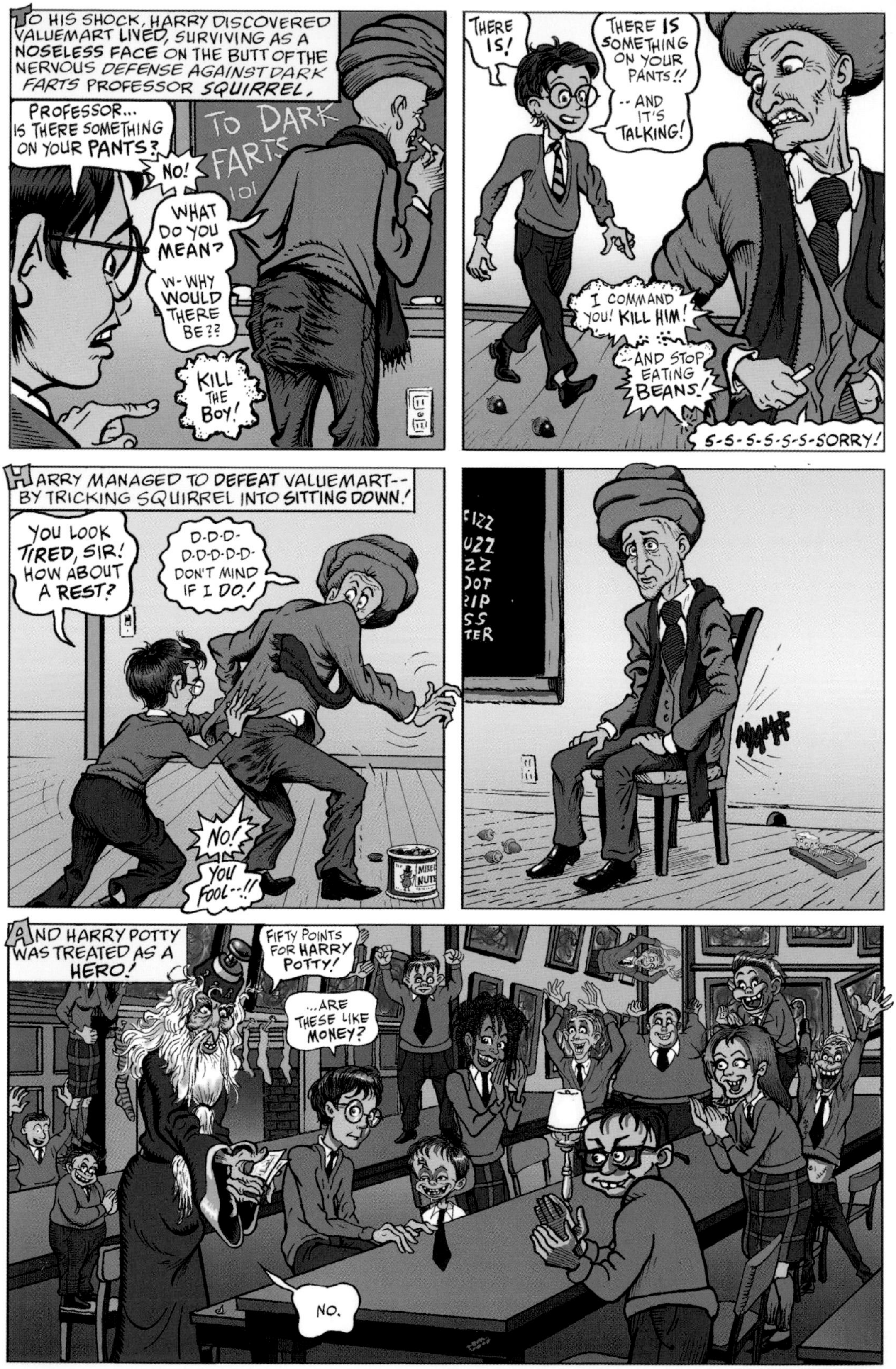
TO HIS SHOCK, HARRY DISCOVERED VALUEMART LIVED, SURVIVING AS A NOSELESS FACE ON THE BUTT OF THE NERVOUS DEFENSE AGAINST DARK FARTS PROFESSOR SQUIRREL.
PROFESSOR... IS THERE SOMETHING ON YOUR PANTS?
TO DARK FARTS 101
NO!
WHAT DO YOU MEAN?
W-WHY WOULD THERE BE??
KILL THE BOY!
THERE IS!
THERE IS SOMETHING ON YOUR PANTS!!
-- AND IT'S TALKING!
I COMMAND YOU! KILL HIM!
--AND STOP EATING BEANS!
S-S-S-S-S-S-SORRY!
HARRY MANAGED TO DEFEAT VALUEMART-- BY TRICKING SQUIRREL INTO SITTING DOWN!
YOU LOOK TIRED, SIR! HOW ABOUT A REST?
D-D-D-D-D-D-D-D- DON'T MIND IF I DO!
NO!
YOU FOOL--!!
MIXED NUTS
MMMFF
AND HARRY POTTY WAS TREATED AS A HERO!
FIFTY POINTS FOR HARRY POTTY!
...ARE THESE LIKE MONEY?
NO.

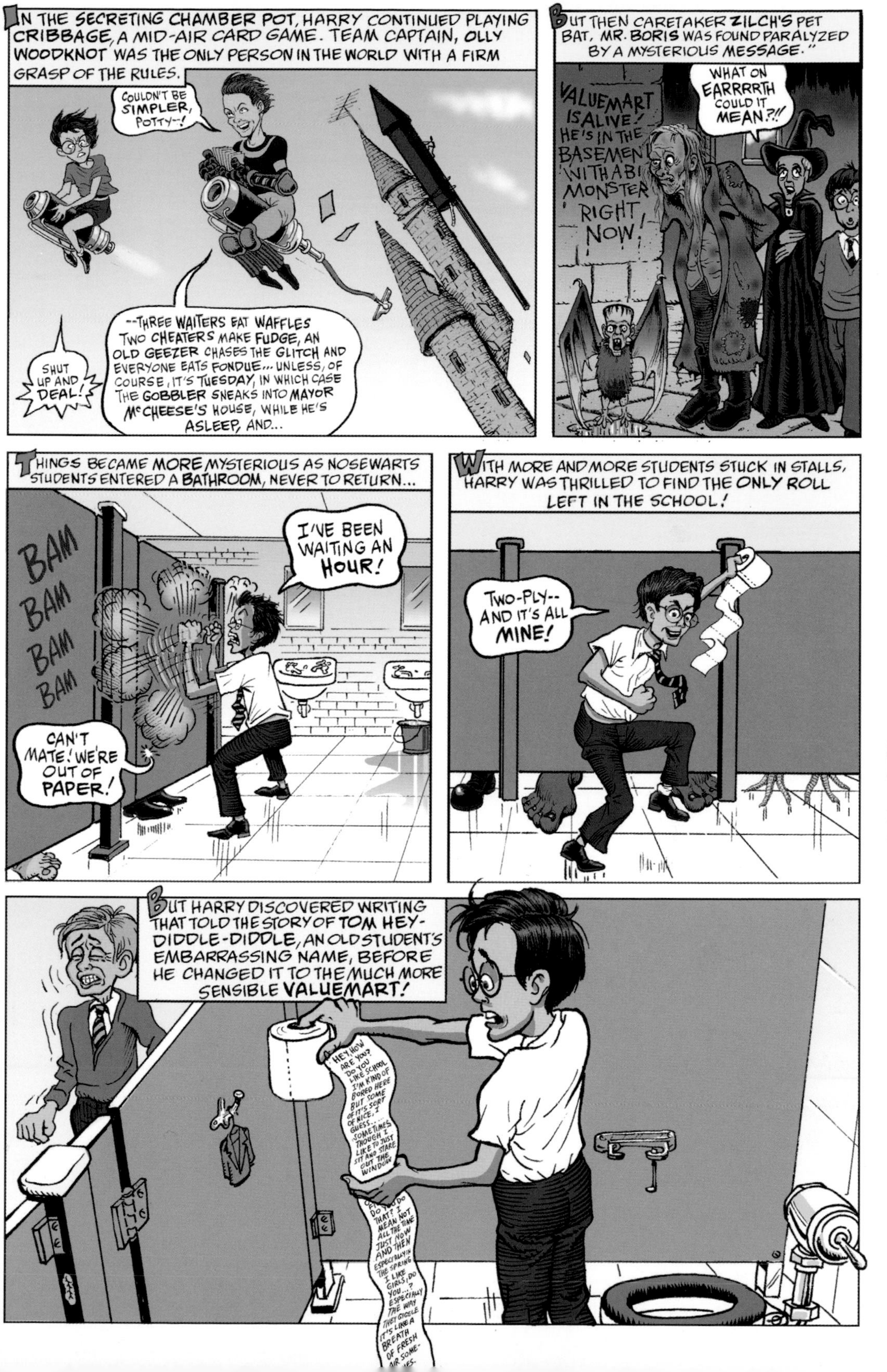
IN THE SECRETING CHAMBER POT, HARRY CONTINUED PLAYING CRIBBAGE, A MID-AIR CARD GAME. TEAM CAPTAIN, OLLY WOODKNOT WAS THE ONLY PERSON IN THE WORLD WITH A FIRM GRASP OF THE RULES.
COULDN'T BE SIMPLER, POTTY--!
--THREE WAITERS EAT WAFFLES TWO CHEATERS MAKE FUDGE, AN OLD GEEZER CHASES THE GLITCH AND EVERYONE EATS FONDUE... UNLESS, OF COURSE, IT'S TUESDAY, IN WHICH CASE THE GOBBLER SNEAKS INTO MAYOR McCHEESE'S HOUSE, WHILE HE'S ASLEEP, AND...
SHUT UP AND DEAL!
BUT THEN CARETAKER ZILCH'S PET BAT, MR. BORIS WAS FOUND PARALYZED BY A MYSTERIOUS MESSAGE."
VALUEMART IS ALIVE! HE'S IN THE BASEMENT WITH A BIG MONSTER RIGHT NOW!
WHAT ON EARRRRTH COULD IT MEAN?!!
THINGS BECAME MORE MYSTERIOUS AS NOSEWARTS STUDENTS ENTERED A BATHROOM, NEVER TO RETURN...
BAM BAM BAM BAM
I'VE BEEN WAITING AN HOUR!
CAN'T MATE! WE'RE OUT OF PAPER!
WITH MORE AND MORE STUDENTS STUCK IN STALLS, HARRY WAS THRILLED TO FIND THE ONLY ROLL LEFT IN THE SCHOOL!
TWO-PLY-- AND IT'S ALL MINE!
BUT HARRY DISCOVERED WRITING THAT TOLD THE STORY OF TOM HEY-DIDDLE-DIDDLE, AN OLD STUDENT'S EMBARRASSING NAME, BEFORE HE CHANGED IT TO THE MUCH MORE SENSIBLE VALUEMART!
HEY, HOW ARE YOU? DO YOU LIKE SCHOOL I'M KIND OF BORED HERE BUT SOME OF IT'S SORT OF NICE, I GUESS... SOMETIMES THOUGH I LIKE TO JUST SIT AND STARE OUT THE WINDOW
DO THAT? I MEAN NOT ALL THE TIME JUST NOW AND THEN ESPECIALLY IN THE SPRING I LIKE GIRLS, DO YOU...? ESPECIALLY THE WAY THEY GIGGLE IT'S LIKE A BREATH OF FRESH AIR SOME-

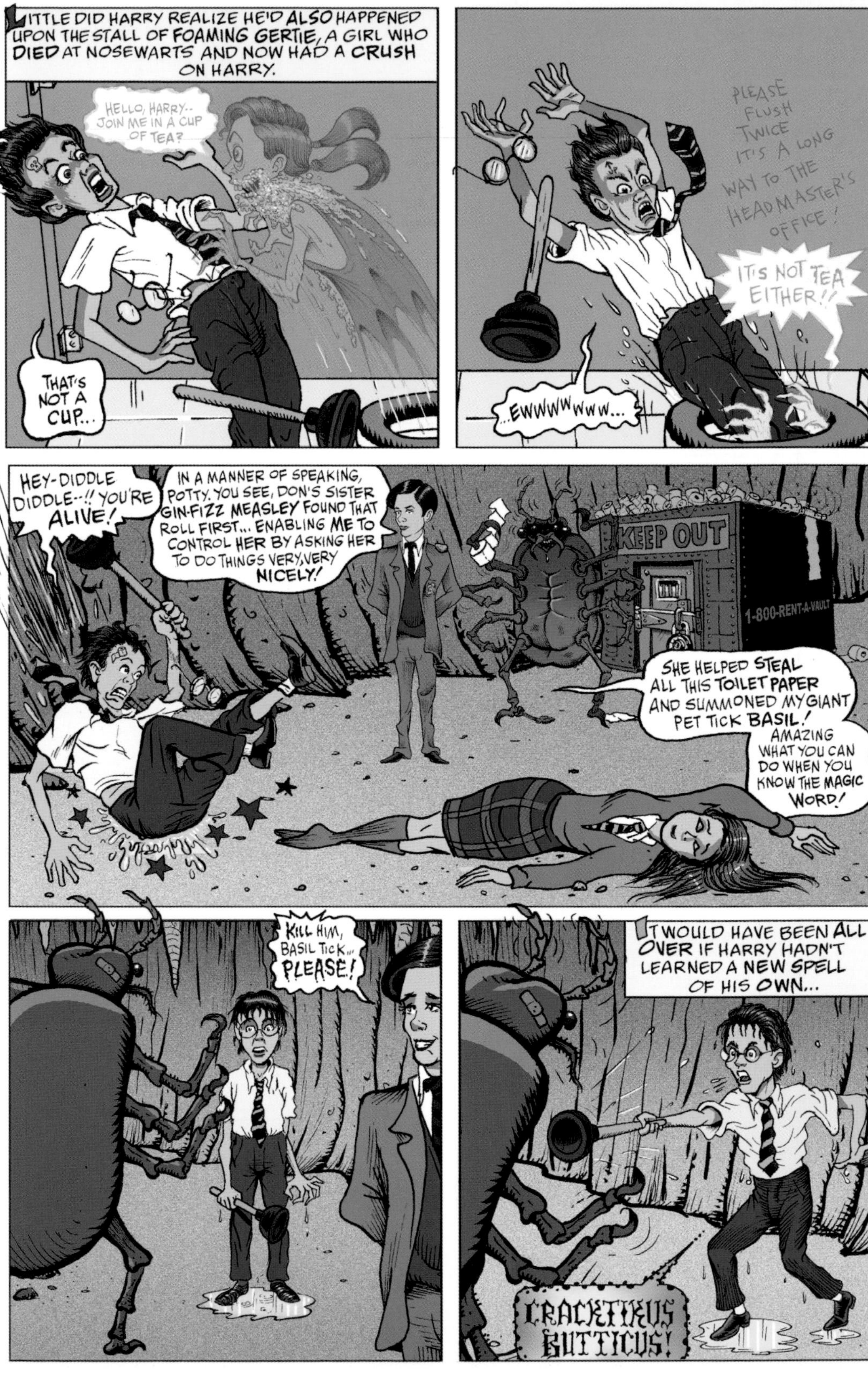
LITTLE DID HARRY REALIZE HE'D ALSO HAPPENED UPON THE STALL OF FOAMING GERTIE, A GIRL WHO DIED AT NOSEWARTS AND NOW HAD A CRUSH ON HARRY.
HELLO, HARRY.. JOIN ME IN A CUP OF TEA?
THAT'S NOT A CUP...
PLEASE FLUSH TWICE IT'S A LONG WAY TO THE HEADMASTER'S OFFICE!
IT'S NOT TEA EITHER!!
...EWWWWWWW...
HEY-DIDDLE DIDDLE--!! YOU'RE ALIVE!
IN A MANNER OF SPEAKING, POTTY. YOU SEE, DON'S SISTER GIN-FIZZ MEASLEY FOUND THAT ROLL FIRST... ENABLING ME TO CONTROL HER BY ASKING HER TO DO THINGS VERY, VERY NICELY!
KEEP OUT
1-800-RENT-A-VAULT
SHE HELPED STEAL ALL THIS TOILET PAPER AND SUMMONED MY GIANT PET TICK BASIL!
AMAZING WHAT YOU CAN DO WHEN YOU KNOW THE MAGIC WORD!
KILL HIM, BASIL TICK... PLEASE!
IT WOULD HAVE BEEN ALL OVER IF HARRY HADN'T LEARNED A NEW SPELL OF HIS OWN...
CRACKTIKUS BUTTICUS!

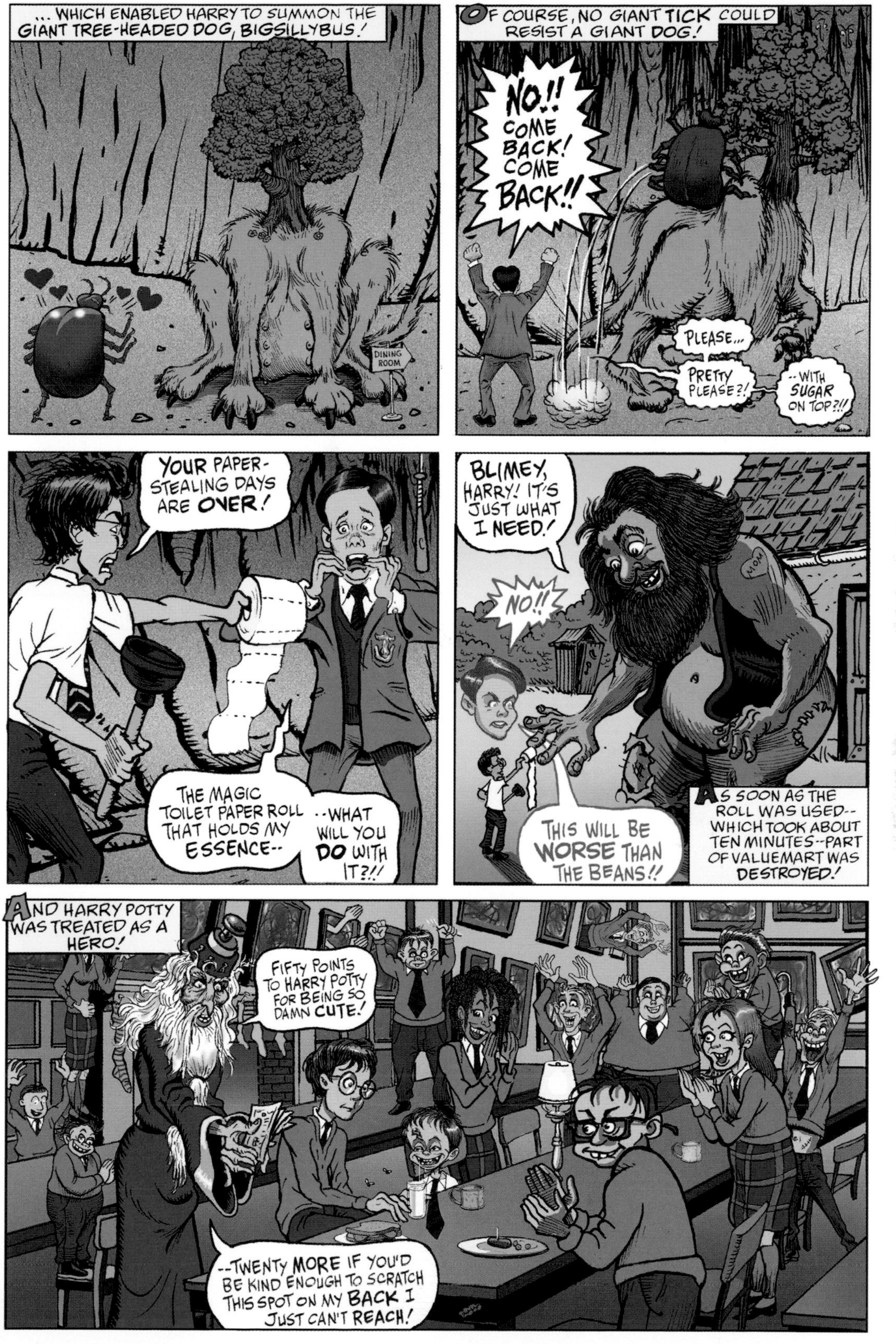
...WHICH ENABLED HARRY TO SUMMON THE GIANT TREE-HEADED DOG, BIGSILLYBUS!
DINING ROOM
OF COURSE, NO GIANT TICK COULD RESIST A GIANT DOG!
NO!! COME BACK! COME BACK!!
PLEASE...
PRETTY PLEASE?!
--WITH SUGAR ON TOP?!!
YOUR PAPER-STEALING DAYS ARE OVER!
THE MAGIC TOILET PAPER ROLL THAT HOLDS MY ESSENCE--
--WHAT WILL YOU DO WITH IT?!!
BLIMEY, HARRY! IT'S JUST WHAT I NEED!
MOM
NO!!
THIS WILL BE WORSE THAN THE BEANS!!
AS SOON AS THE ROLL WAS USED--WHICH TOOK ABOUT TEN MINUTES--PART OF VALUEMART WAS DESTROYED!
AND HARRY POTTY WAS TREATED AS A HERO!
FIFTY POINTS TO HARRY POTTY FOR BEING SO DAMN CUTE!
--TWENTY MORE IF YOU'D BE KIND ENOUGH TO SCRATCH THIS SPOT ON MY BACK I JUST CAN'T REACH!

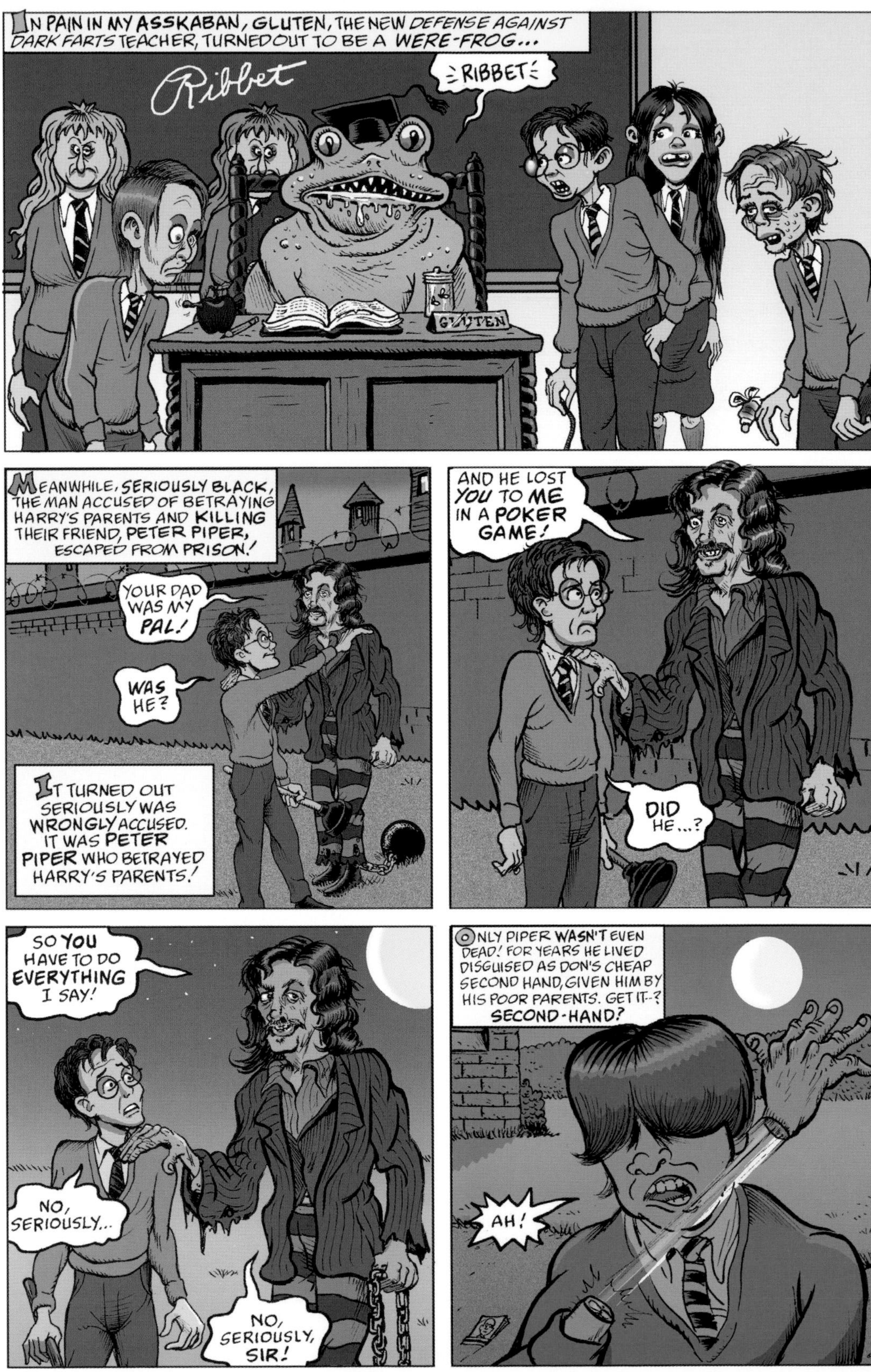
IN PAIN IN MY ASSKABAN, GLUTEN, THE NEW DEFENSE AGAINST DARK FARTS TEACHER, TURNED OUT TO BE A WERE-FROG...
Ribbet
RIBBET
GLUTEN
MEANWHILE, SERIOUSLY BLACK, THE MAN ACCUSED OF BETRAYING HARRY'S PARENTS AND KILLING THEIR FRIEND, PETER PIPER, ESCAPED FROM PRISON!
YOUR DAD WAS MY PAL!
WAS HE?
IT TURNED OUT SERIOUSLY WAS WRONGLY ACCUSED. IT WAS PETER PIPER WHO BETRAYED HARRY'S PARENTS!
AND HE LOST YOU TO ME IN A POKER GAME!
DID HE...?
SO YOU HAVE TO DO EVERYTHING I SAY!
NO, SERIOUSLY...
NO, SERIOUSLY, SIR!
ONLY PIPER WASN'T EVEN DEAD! FOR YEARS HE LIVED DISGUISED AS DON'S CHEAP SECOND HAND, GIVEN HIM BY HIS POOR PARENTS. GET IT--? SECOND-HAND?
AH!

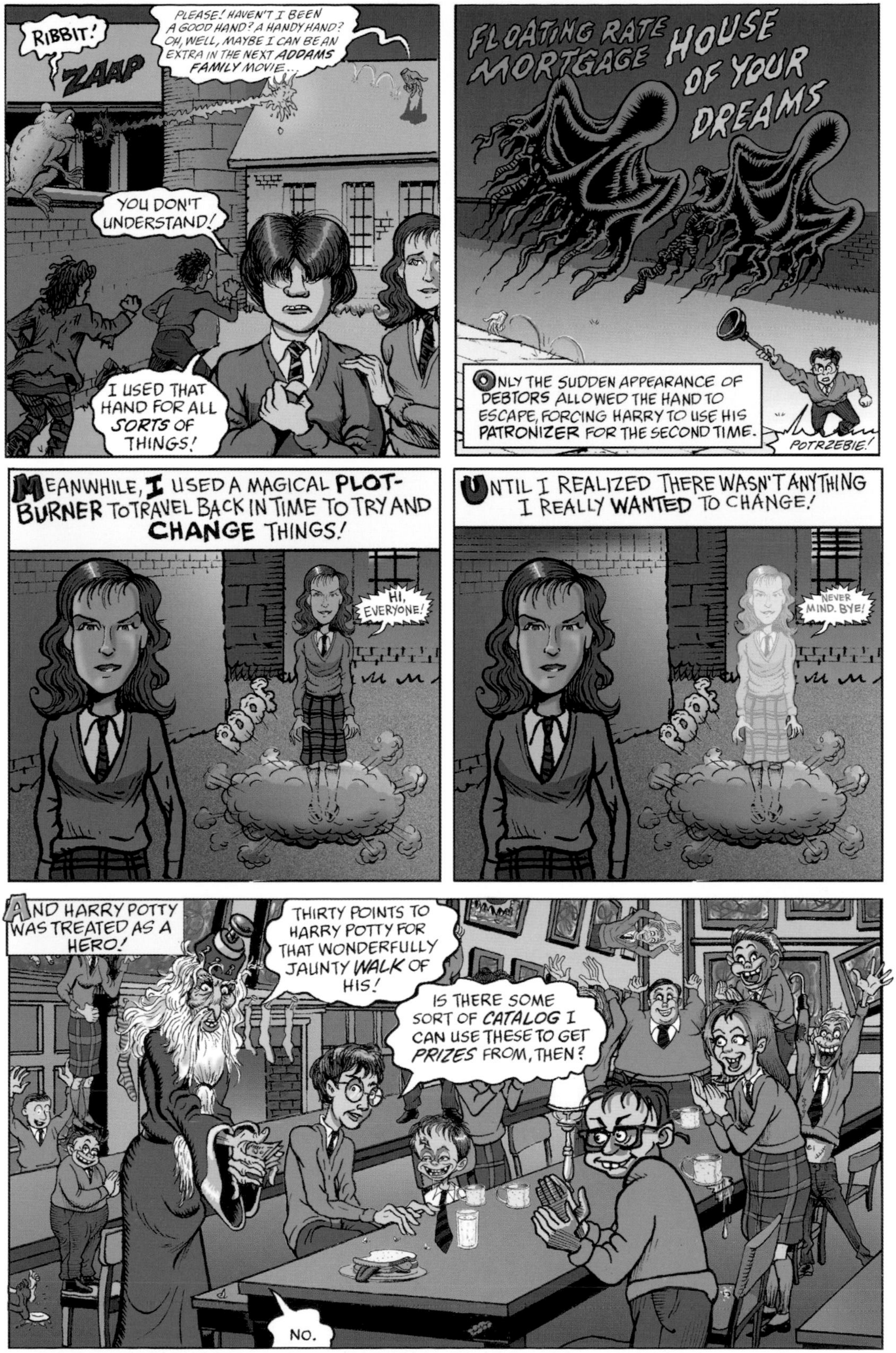
RIBBIT!
ZAAP
PLEASE! HAVEN'T I BEEN A GOOD HAND? A HANDY HAND? OH, WELL, MAYBE I CAN BE AN EXTRA IN THE NEXT ADDAMS FAMILY MOVIE...
YOU DON'T UNDERSTAND!
I USED THAT HAND FOR ALL SORTS OF THINGS!
FLOATING RATE MORTGAGE
HOUSE OF YOUR DREAMS
ONLY THE SUDDEN APPEARANCE OF DEBTORS ALLOWED THE HAND TO ESCAPE, FORCING HARRY TO USE HIS PATRONIZER FOR THE SECOND TIME.
POTRZEBIE!
MEANWHILE, I USED A MAGICAL PLOT-BURNER TO TRAVEL BACK IN TIME TO TRY AND CHANGE THINGS!
HI, EVERYONE!
POOF
UNTIL I REALIZED THERE WASN'T ANYTHING I REALLY WANTED TO CHANGE!
NEVER MIND. BYE!
POOF
AND HARRY POTTY WAS TREATED AS A HERO!
THIRTY POINTS TO HARRY POTTY FOR THAT WONDERFULLY JAUNTY WALK OF HIS!
IS THERE SOME SORT OF CATALOG I CAN USE THESE TO GET PRIZES FROM, THEN?
NO.

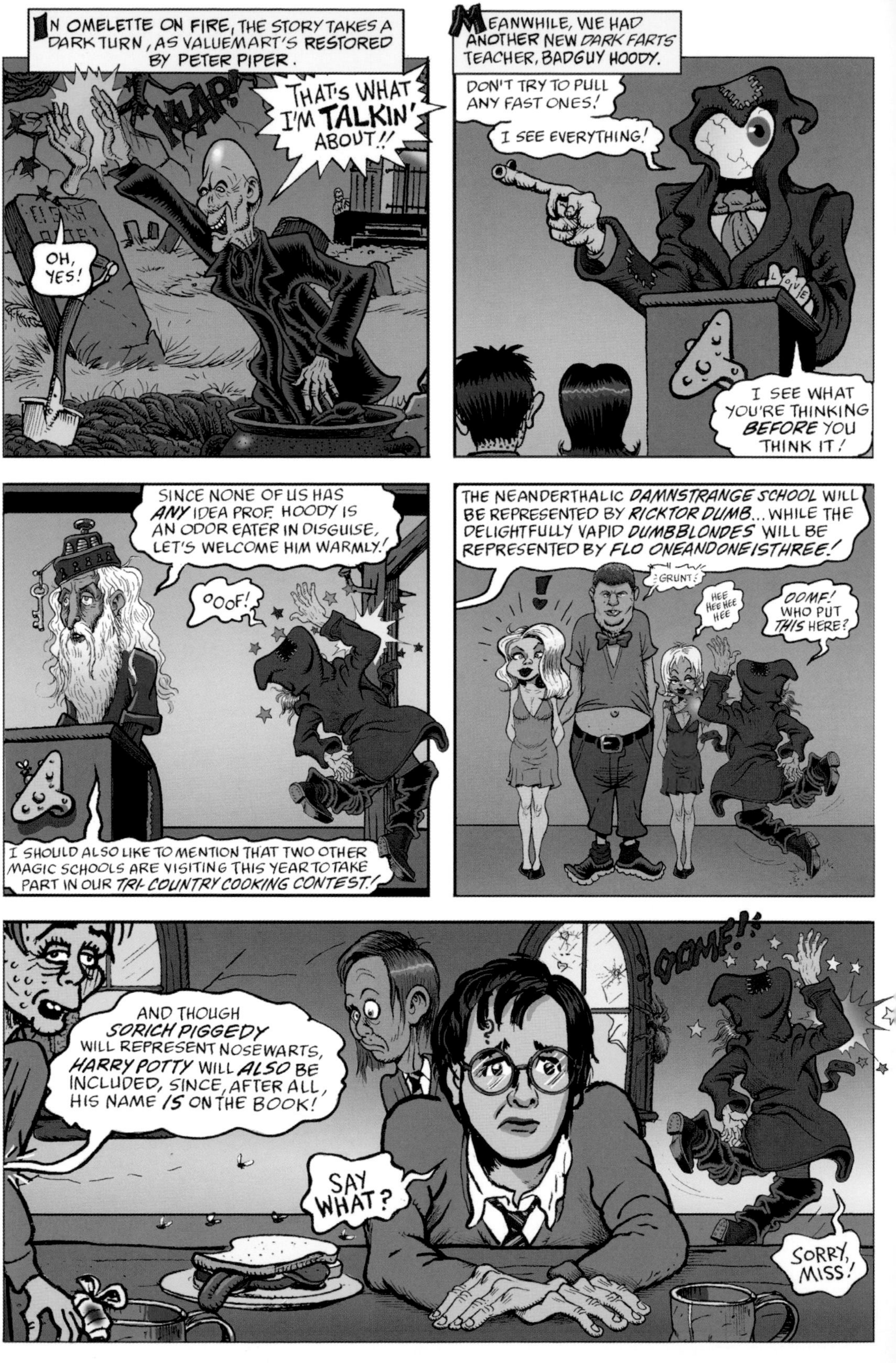
IN OMELETTE ON FIRE, THE STORY TAKES A DARK TURN, AS VALUEMART'S RESTORED BY PETER PIPER.
KLAP!
THAT'S WHAT I'M TALKIN' ABOUT!!
OH, YES!
MEANWHILE, WE HAD ANOTHER NEW DARK FARTS TEACHER, BADGUY HOODY.
DON'T TRY TO PULL ANY FAST ONES!
I SEE EVERYTHING!
I SEE WHAT YOU'RE THINKING BEFORE YOU THINK IT!
SINCE NONE OF US HAS ANY IDEA PROF. HOODY IS AN ODOR EATER IN DISGUISE, LET'S WELCOME HIM WARMLY!
OOOF!
I SHOULD ALSO LIKE TO MENTION THAT TWO OTHER MAGIC SCHOOLS ARE VISITING THIS YEAR TO TAKE PART IN OUR TRI-COUNTRY COOKING CONTEST!
THE NEANDERTHALIC DAMNSTRANGE SCHOOL WILL BE REPRESENTED BY RICKTOR DUMB... WHILE THE DELIGHTFULLY VAPID DUMBBLONDES WILL BE REPRESENTED BY FLO ONEANDONEISTHREE!
!
GRUNT!
HEE HEE HEE HEE
OOMF! WHO PUT THIS HERE?
AND THOUGH SORICH PIGGEDY WILL REPRESENT NOSEWARTS, HARRY POTTY WILL ALSO BE INCLUDED, SINCE, AFTER ALL, HIS NAME IS ON THE BOOK!
OOMF!!
SAY WHAT?
SORRY, MISS!

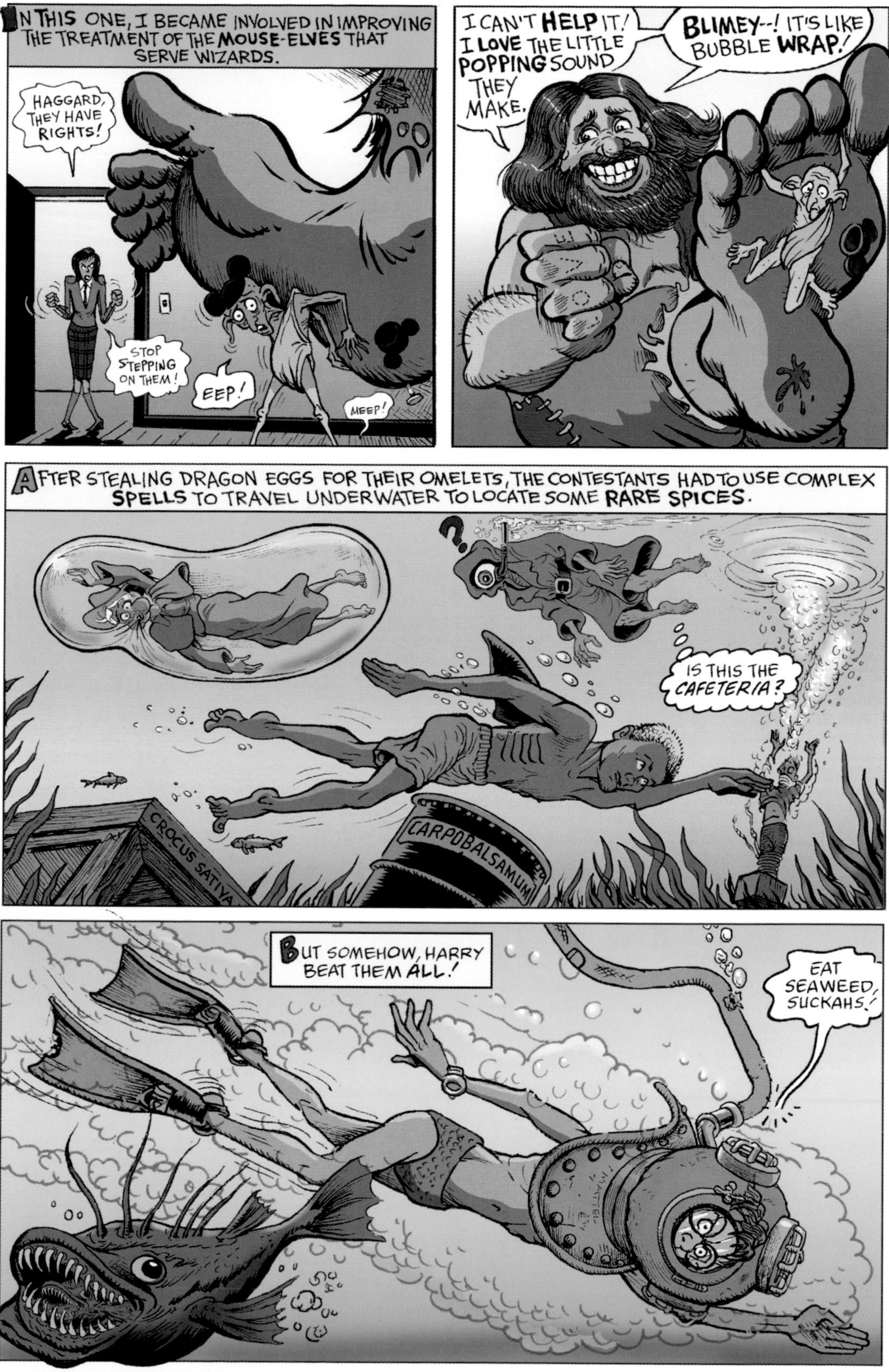
IN THIS ONE, I BECAME INVOLVED IN IMPROVING THE TREATMENT OF THE MOUSE-ELVES THAT SERVE WIZARDS.
HAGGARD, THEY HAVE RIGHTS!
STOP STEPPING ON THEM!
EEP!
MEEP!
I CAN'T HELP IT! I LOVE THE LITTLE POPPING SOUND THEY MAKE.
BLIMEY--! IT'S LIKE BUBBLE WRAP!
AFTER STEALING DRAGON EGGS FOR THEIR OMELETS, THE CONTESTANTS HAD TO USE COMPLEX SPELLS TO TRAVEL UNDERWATER TO LOCATE SOME RARE SPICES.
?
IS THIS THE CAFETERIA?
CROCUS SATIVA
CARPOBALSAMUM
BUT SOMEHOW, HARRY BEAT THEM ALL!
EAT SEAWEED, SUCKAHS!

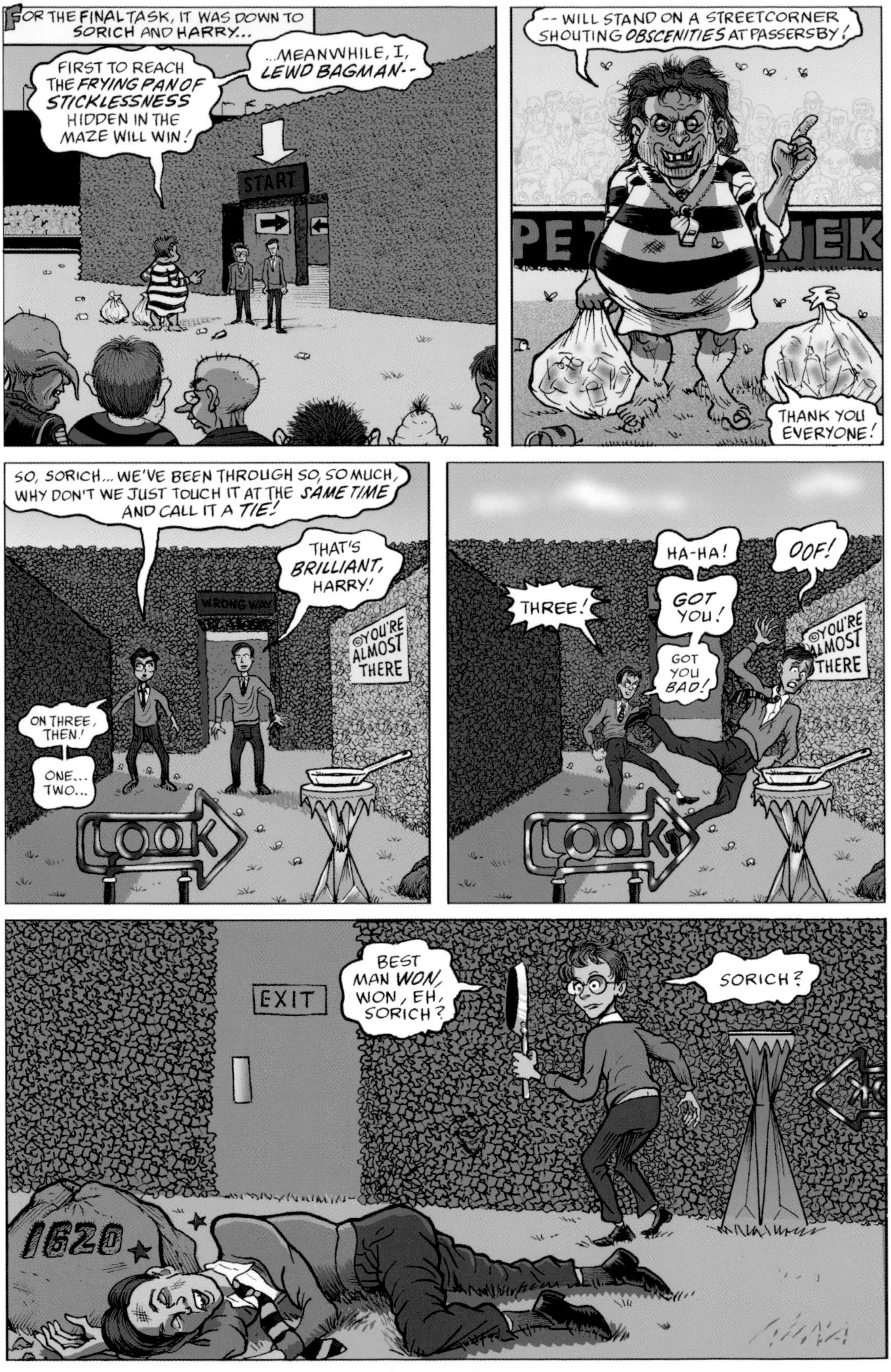
FOR THE FINAL TASK, IT WAS DOWN TO SORICH AND HARRY...
FIRST TO REACH THE FRYING PAN OF STICKLESSNESS HIDDEN IN THE MAZE WILL WIN!
...MEANWHILE, I, LEWD BAGMAN--
START
-- WILL STAND ON A STREETCORNER SHOUTING OBSCENITIES AT PASSERSBY!
THANK YOU EVERYONE!
SO, SORICH... WE'VE BEEN THROUGH SO, SO MUCH, WHY DON'T WE JUST TOUCH IT AT THE SAME TIME AND CALL IT A TIE!
THAT'S BRILLIANT, HARRY!
WRONG WAY
YOU'RE ALMOST THERE
ON THREE, THEN!
ONE... TWO...
LOOK
THREE!
HA-HA!
GOT YOU!
GOT YOU BAD!
OOF!
YOU'RE ALMOST THERE
LOOK
EXIT
BEST MAN WON, WON, EH, SORICH?
SORICH?
1620

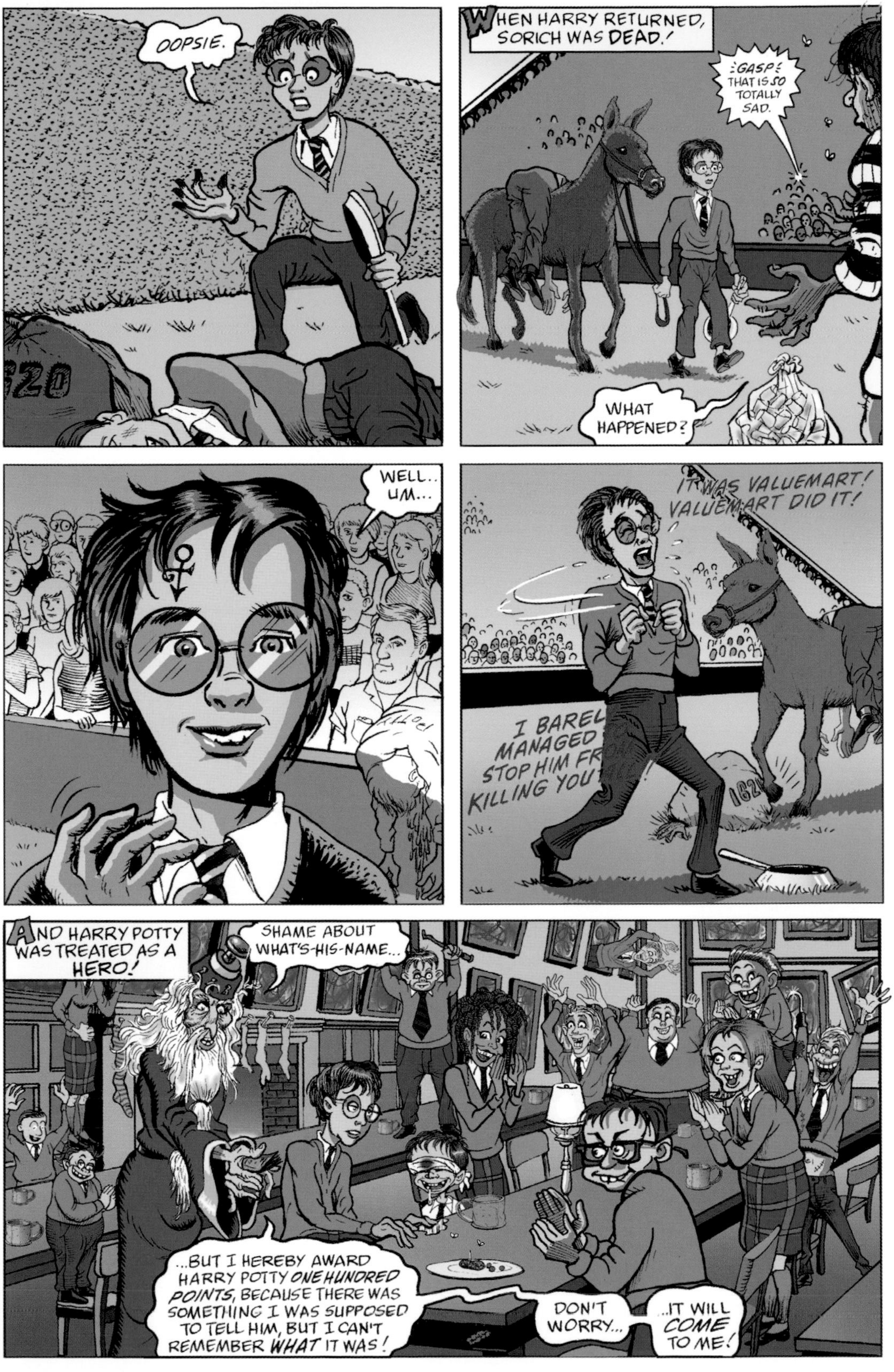
OOPSIE.
WHEN HARRY RETURNED, SORICH WAS DEAD!
GASP THAT IS SO TOTALLY SAD.
WHAT HAPPENED?
WELL.. UM...
IT WAS VALUEMART! VALUEMART DID IT!
I BAREL MANAGED STOP HIM FR KILLING YOU
AND HARRY POTTY WAS TREATED AS A HERO!
SHAME ABOUT WHAT'S-HIS-NAME...
...BUT I HEREBY AWARD HARRY POTTY ONE HUNDRED POINTS, BECAUSE THERE WAS SOMETHING I WAS SUPPOSED TO TELL HIM, BUT I CAN'T REMEMBER WHAT IT WAS!
DON'T WORRY...
...IT WILL COME TO ME!

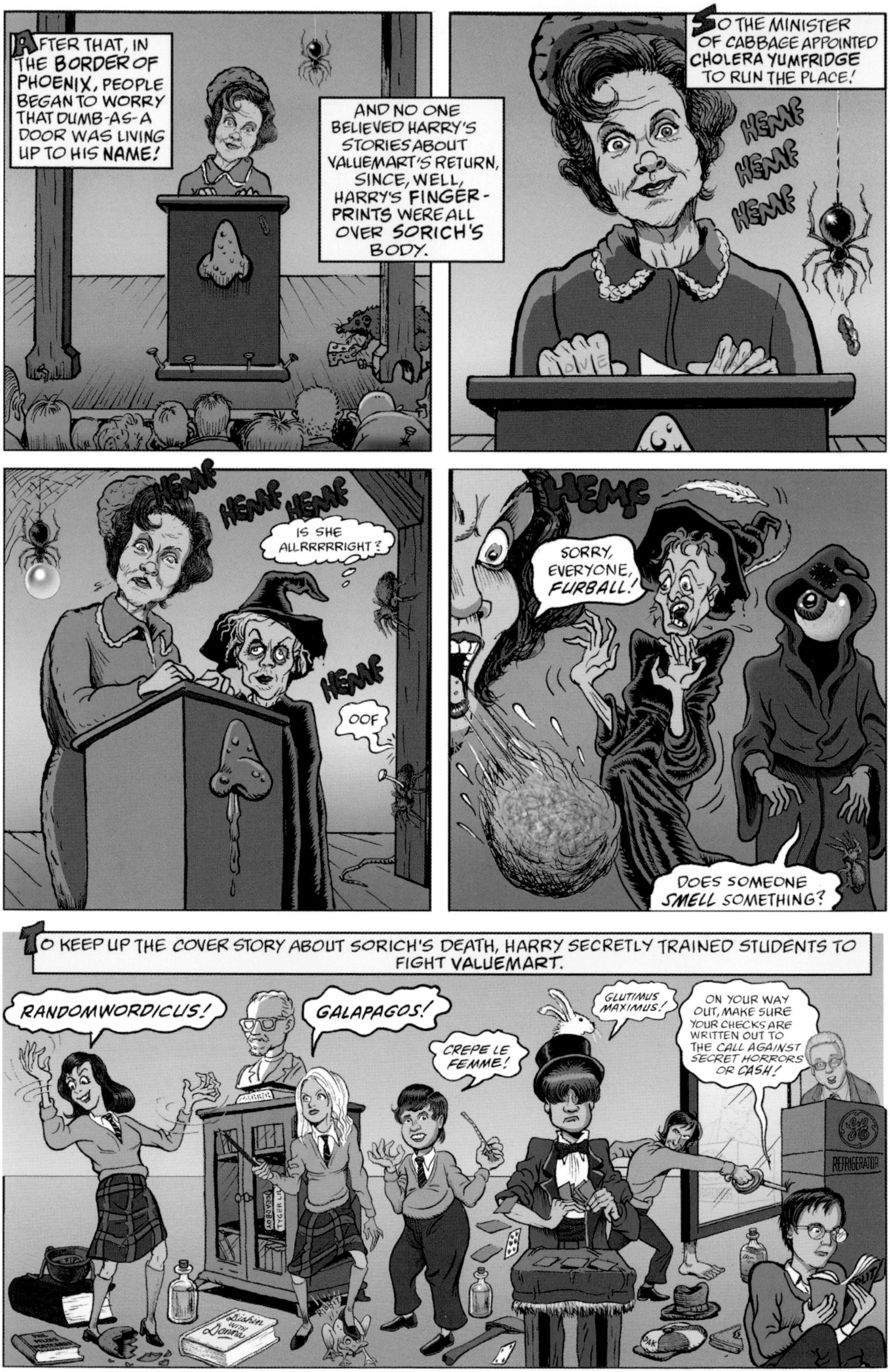
AFTER THAT, IN THE BORDER OF PHOENIX, PEOPLE BEGAN TO WORRY THAT DUMB-AS-A DOOR WAS LIVING UP TO HIS NAME!
AND NO ONE BELIEVED HARRY'S STORIES ABOUT VALUEMART'S RETURN, SINCE, WELL, HARRY'S FINGER-PRINTS WERE ALL OVER SORICH'S BODY.
SO THE MINISTER OF CABBAGE APPOINTED CHOLERA YUMFRIDGE TO RUN THE PLACE!
HEMF
HEMF
HEMF
HEMF
HEMF HEMF
IS SHE ALLRRRRRIGHT?
HEMF
OOF
HEMF
SORRY, EVERYONE, FURBALL!
DOES SOMEONE SMELL SOMETHING?
TO KEEP UP THE COVER STORY ABOUT SORICH'S DEATH, HARRY SECRETLY TRAINED STUDENTS TO FIGHT VALUEMART.
RANDOMWORDICUS!
GALAPAGOS!
CREPE LE FEMME!
GLUTIMUS MAXIMUS!
ON YOUR WAY OUT, MAKE SURE YOUR CHECKS ARE WRITTEN OUT TO THE CALL AGAINST SECRET HORRORS OR CASH!
RIBBIT
Dishin with Donna
REFRIGERATOR

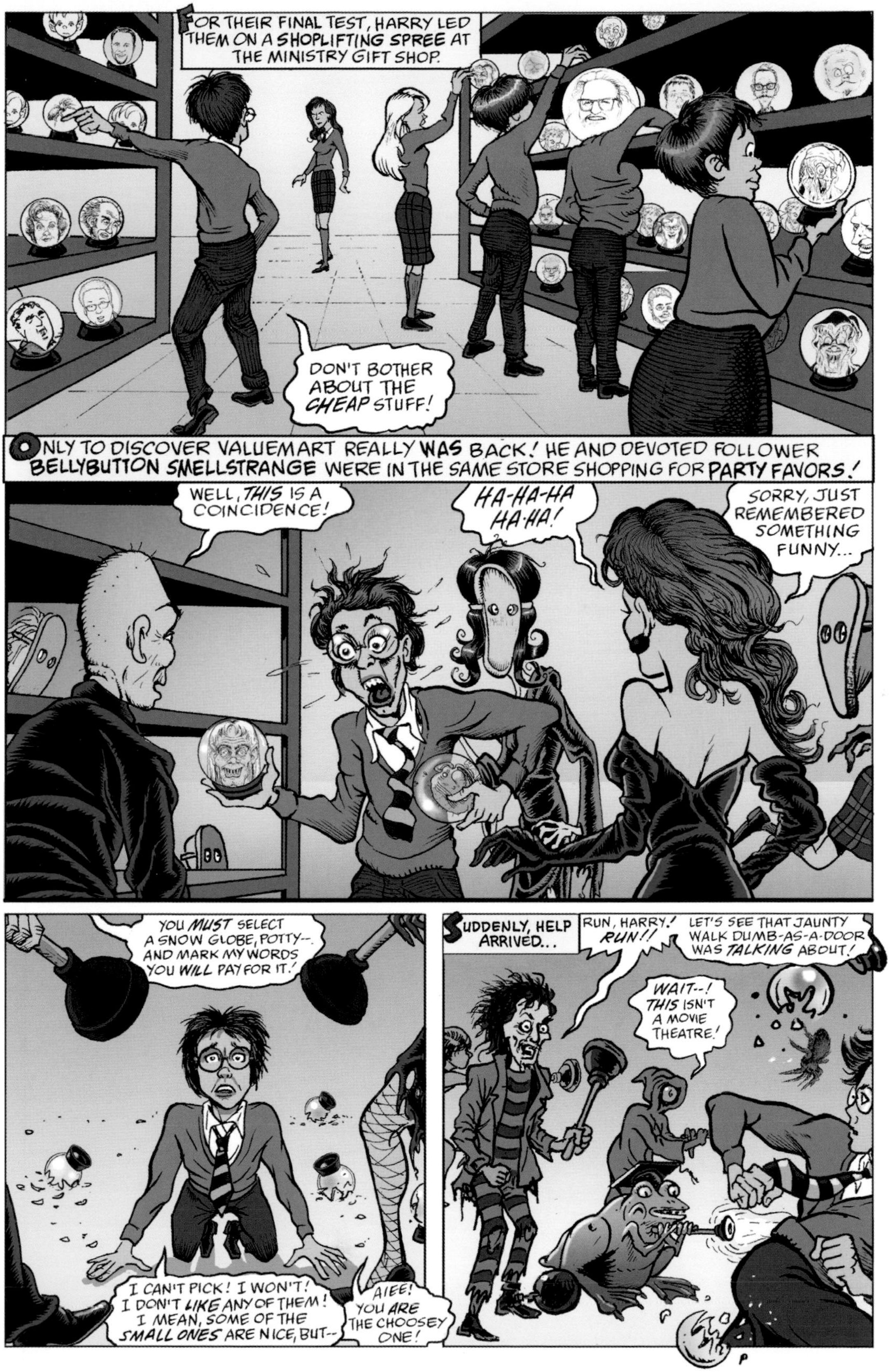
FOR THEIR FINAL TEST, HARRY LED THEM ON A SHOPLIFTING SPREE AT THE MINISTRY GIFT SHOP.
DON'T BOTHER ABOUT THE CHEAP STUFF!
ONLY TO DISCOVER VALUEMART REALLY WAS BACK! HE AND DEVOTED FOLLOWER BELLYBUTTON SMELLSTRANGE WERE IN THE SAME STORE SHOPPING FOR PARTY FAVORS!
WELL, THIS IS A COINCIDENCE!
HA-HA-HA HA-HA!
SORRY, JUST REMEMBERED SOMETHING FUNNY...
YOU MUST SELECT A SNOW GLOBE, POTTY-- AND MARK MY WORDS YOU WILL PAY FOR IT.
I CAN'T PICK! I WON'T! I DON'T LIKE ANY OF THEM! I MEAN, SOME OF THE SMALL ONES ARE NICE, BUT--
AIEE! YOU ARE THE CHOOSEY ONE!
SUDDENLY, HELP ARRIVED...
RUN, HARRY! RUN!!
LET'S SEE THAT JAUNTY WALK DUMB-AS-A-DOOR WAS TALKING ABOUT!
WAIT--! THIS ISN'T A MOVIE THEATRE!

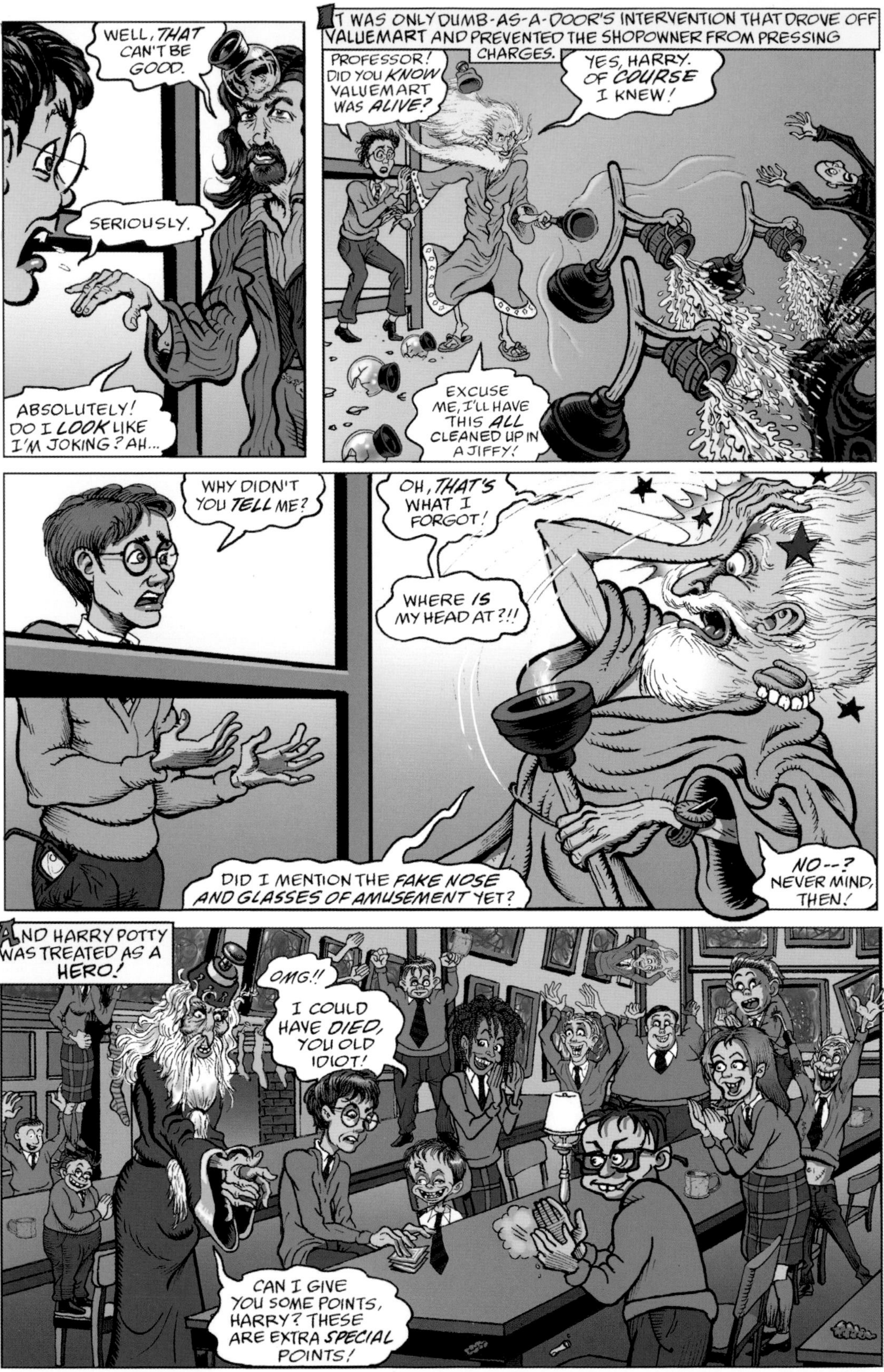
WELL, THAT CAN'T BE GOOD.
SERIOUSLY.
ABSOLUTELY! DO I LOOK LIKE I'M JOKING? AH...
IT WAS ONLY DUMB-AS-A-DOOR'S INTERVENTION THAT DROVE OFF VALUEMART AND PREVENTED THE SHOPOWNER FROM PRESSING CHARGES.
PROFESSOR! DID YOU KNOW VALUEMART WAS ALIVE?
YES, HARRY. OF COURSE I KNEW!
EXCUSE ME, I'LL HAVE THIS ALL CLEANED UP IN A JIFFY!
WHY DIDN'T YOU TELL ME?
OH, THAT'S WHAT I FORGOT!
WHERE IS MY HEAD AT?!!
DID I MENTION THE FAKE NOSE AND GLASSES OF AMUSEMENT YET?
NO--? NEVER MIND, THEN!
AND HARRY POTTY WAS TREATED AS A HERO!
OMG!! I COULD HAVE DIED, YOU OLD IDIOT!
CAN I GIVE YOU SOME POINTS, HARRY? THESE ARE EXTRA SPECIAL POINTS!

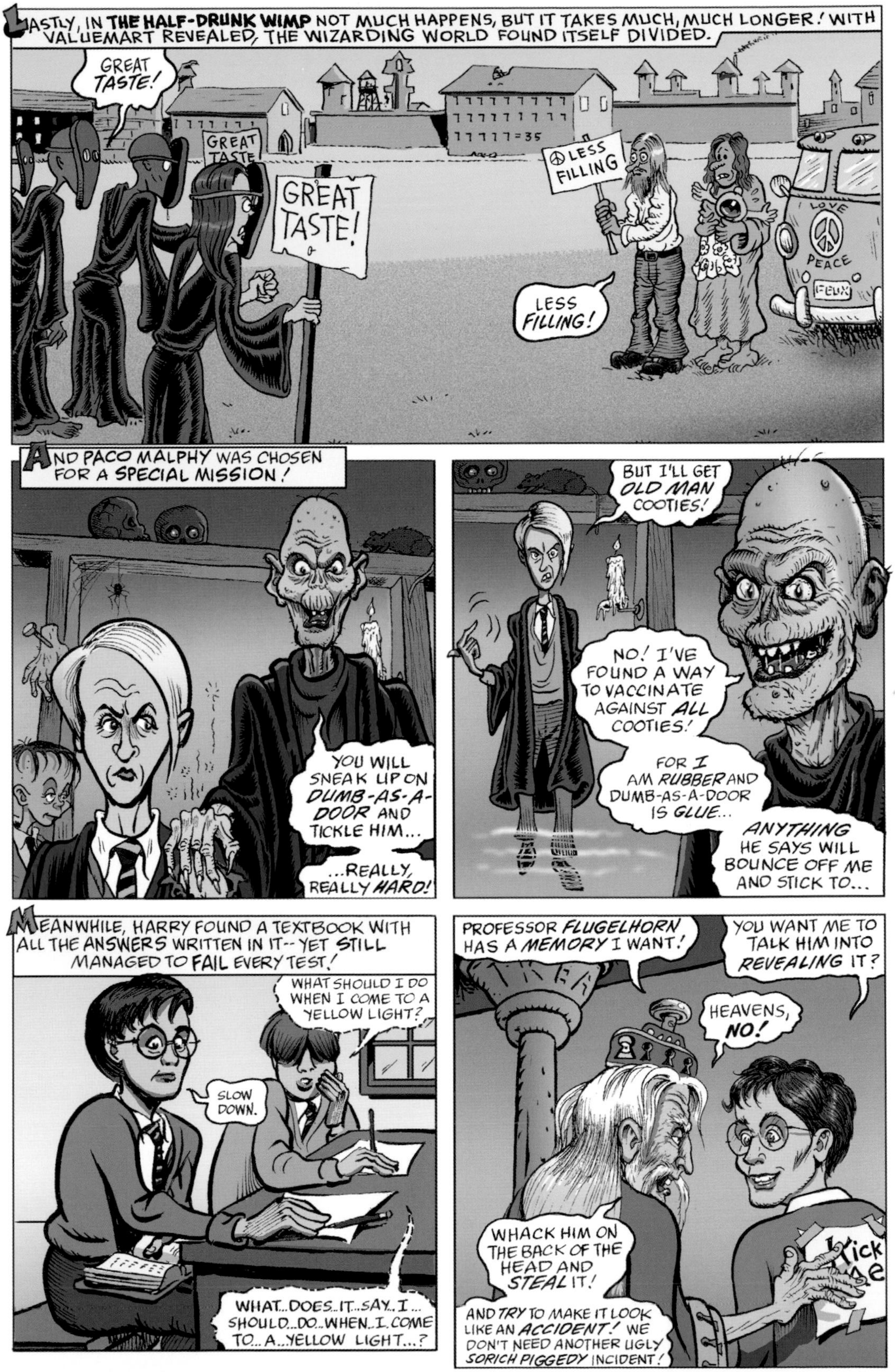
LASTLY, IN THE HALF-DRUNK WIMP NOT MUCH HAPPENS, BUT IT TAKES MUCH, MUCH LONGER! WITH VALUEMART REVEALED, THE WIZARDING WORLD FOUND ITSELF DIVIDED.
GREAT TASTE!
GREAT TASTE
GREAT TASTE!
LESS FILLING
LOVE
PEACE
LESS FILLING!
AND PACO MALPHY WAS CHOSEN FOR A SPECIAL MISSION!
YOU WILL SNEAK UP ON DUMB-AS-A-DOOR AND TICKLE HIM...
...REALLY, REALLY HARD!
BUT I'LL GET OLD MAN COOTIES!
NO! I'VE FOUND A WAY TO VACCINATE AGAINST ALL COOTIES!
FOR I AM RUBBER AND DUMB-AS-A-DOOR IS GLUE...
ANYTHING HE SAYS WILL BOUNCE OFF ME AND STICK TO...
MEANWHILE, HARRY FOUND A TEXTBOOK WITH ALL THE ANSWERS WRITTEN IN IT-- YET STILL MANAGED TO FAIL EVERY TEST!
WHAT SHOULD I DO WHEN I COME TO A YELLOW LIGHT?
SLOW DOWN.
WHAT...DOES...IT...SAY...I... SHOULD...DO...WHEN...I...COME TO...A...YELLOW LIGHT...?
PROFESSOR FLUGELHORN HAS A MEMORY I WANT!
YOU WANT ME TO TALK HIM INTO REVEALING IT?
HEAVENS, NO!
WHACK HIM ON THE BACK OF THE HEAD AND STEAL IT!
AND TRY TO MAKE IT LOOK LIKE AN ACCIDENT! WE DON'T NEED ANOTHER UGLY SORICH PIGGEDY INCIDENT!

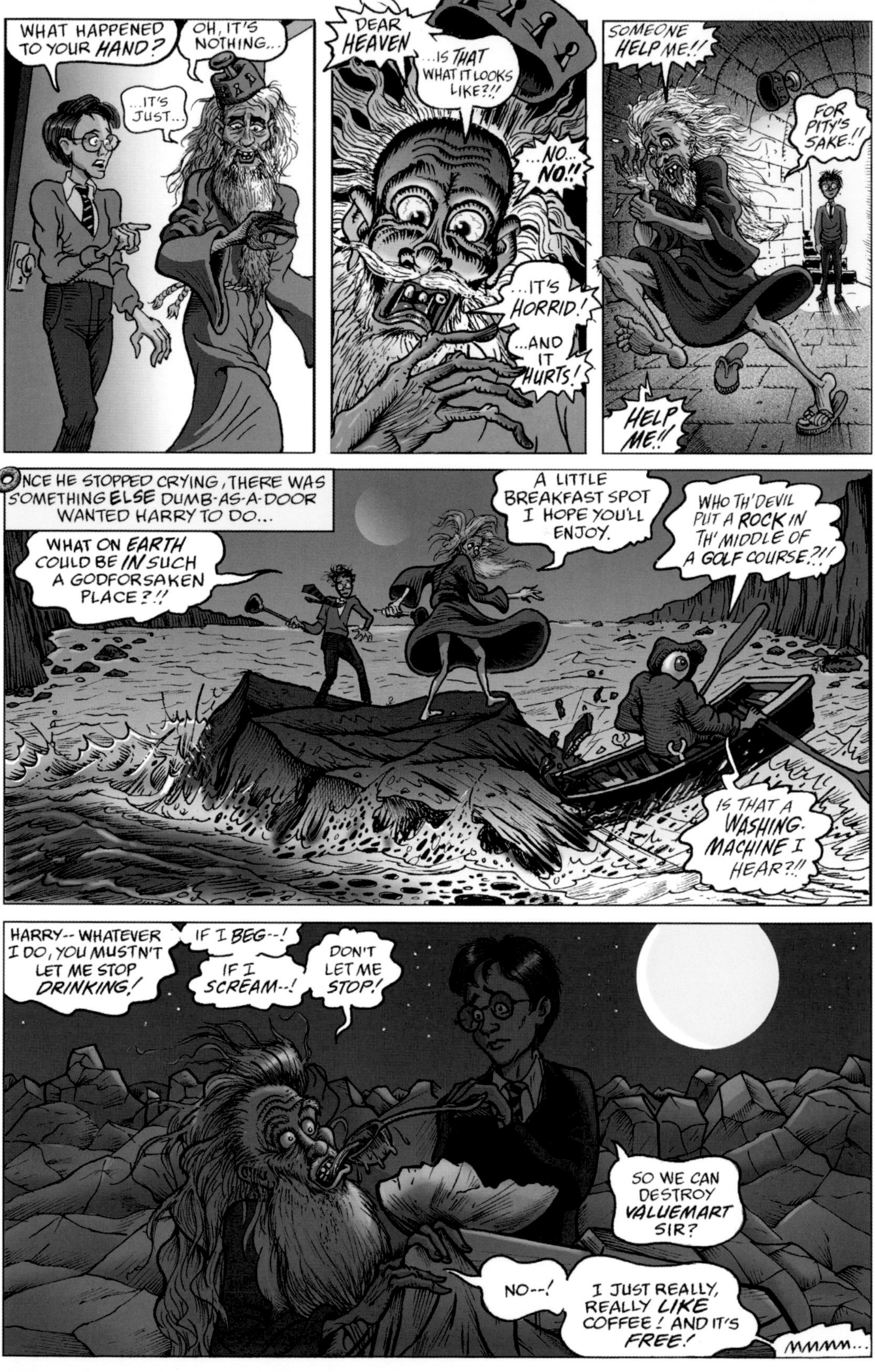
WHAT HAPPENED TO YOUR HAND?
OH, IT'S NOTHING...
...IT'S JUST...
DEAR HEAVEN
...IS THAT WHAT IT LOOKS LIKE?!!
...NO... NO!!
...IT'S HORRID!
...AND IT HURTS!
SOMEONE HELP ME!!
FOR PITY'S SAKE!!
HELP ME!!
ONCE HE STOPPED CRYING, THERE WAS SOMETHING ELSE DUMB-AS-A-DOOR WANTED HARRY TO DO...
WHAT ON EARTH COULD BE IN SUCH A GODFORSAKEN PLACE?!!
A LITTLE BREAKFAST SPOT I HOPE YOU'LL ENJOY.
WHO TH'DEVIL PUT A ROCK IN TH' MIDDLE OF A GOLF COURSE?!!
IS THAT A WASHING-MACHINE I HEAR?!!
HARRY-- WHATEVER I DO, YOU MUSTN'T LET ME STOP DRINKING!
IF I BEG--!
IF I SCREAM--!
DON'T LET ME STOP!
SO WE CAN DESTROY VALUEMART SIR?
NO--!
I JUST REALLY, REALLY LIKE COFFEE! AND IT'S FREE!
MMMM...

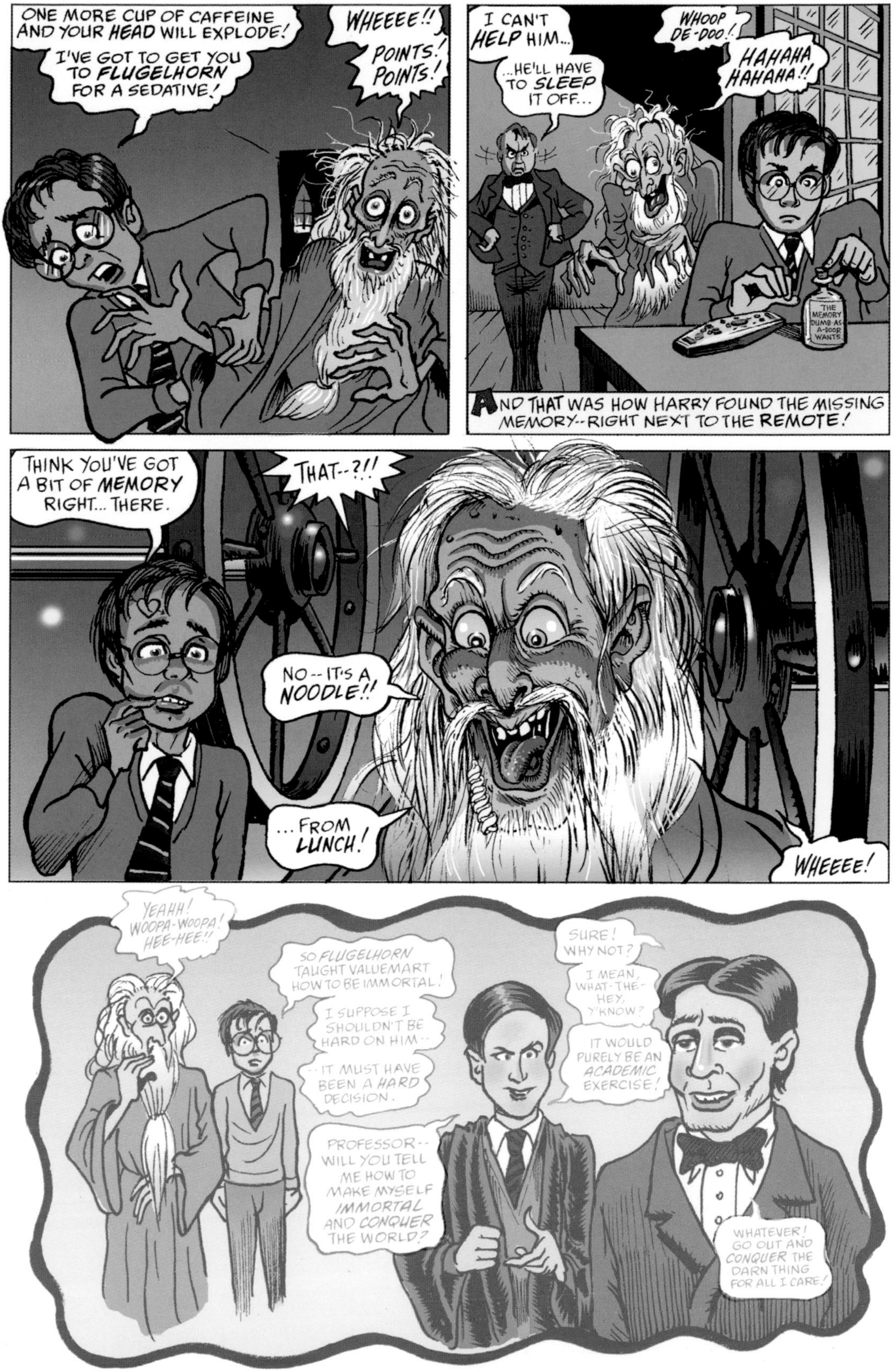
ONE MORE CUP OF CAFFEINE AND YOUR HEAD WILL EXPLODE!
I'VE GOT TO GET YOU TO FLUGELHORN FOR A SEDATIVE!
WHEEEE!!
POINTS! POINTS!
I CAN'T HELP HIM...
...HE'LL HAVE TO SLEEP IT OFF...
WHOOP DE-DOO!
HAHAHA HAHAHA!!
THE MEMORY DUMB-AS-A-DOOR WANTS
AND THAT WAS HOW HARRY FOUND THE MISSING MEMORY--RIGHT NEXT TO THE REMOTE!
THINK YOU'VE GOT A BIT OF MEMORY RIGHT... THERE.
THAT--?!!
NO--IT'S A NOODLE!!
...FROM LUNCH!
WHEEEE!
YEAHH! WOOPA-WOOPA! HEE-HEE!!
SO FLUGELHORN TAUGHT VALUEMART HOW TO BE IMMORTAL!
I SUPPOSE I SHOULDN'T BE HARD ON HIM--
--IT MUST HAVE BEEN A HARD DECISION.
PROFESSOR--WILL YOU TELL ME HOW TO MAKE MYSELF IMMORTAL AND CONQUER THE WORLD?
SURE! WHY NOT?
I MEAN, WHAT-THE-HEY, Y'KNOW?
IT WOULD PURELY BE AN ACADEMIC EXERCISE!
WHATEVER! GO OUT AND CONQUER THE DARN THING FOR ALL I CARE!

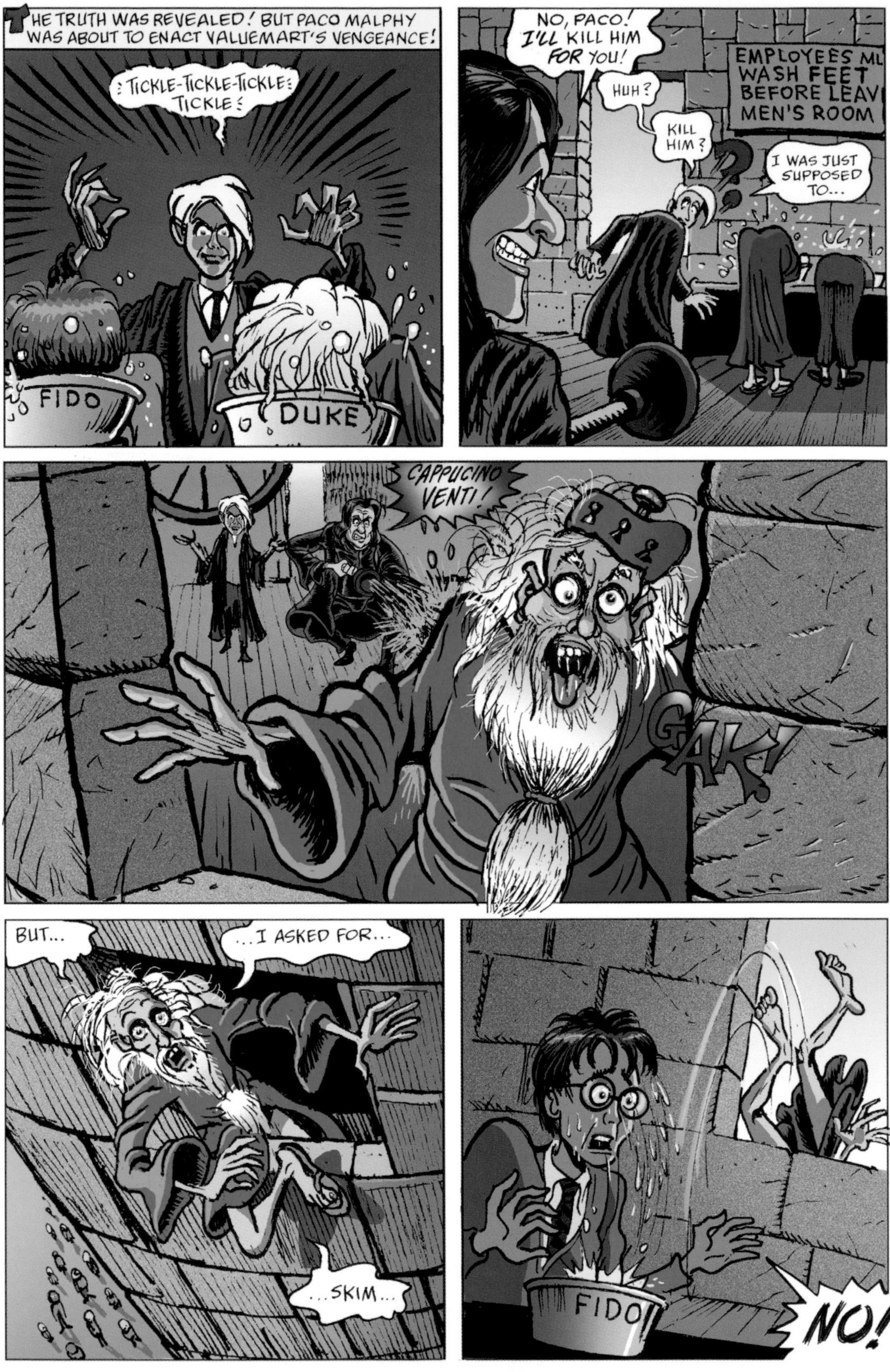
THE TRUTH WAS REVEALED! BUT PACO MALPHY WAS ABOUT TO ENACT VALUEMART'S VENGEANCE!
TICKLE-TICKLE-TICKLE-TICKLE!
FIDO
DUKE
NO, PACO! I'LL KILL HIM FOR YOU!
HUH?
KILL HIM?
I WAS JUST SUPPOSED TO...
EMPLOYEES MU WASH FEET BEFORE LEAV MEN'S ROOM
CAPPUCINO VENTI!
GAK!
BUT...
...I ASKED FOR...
...SKIM...
FIDO
NO!

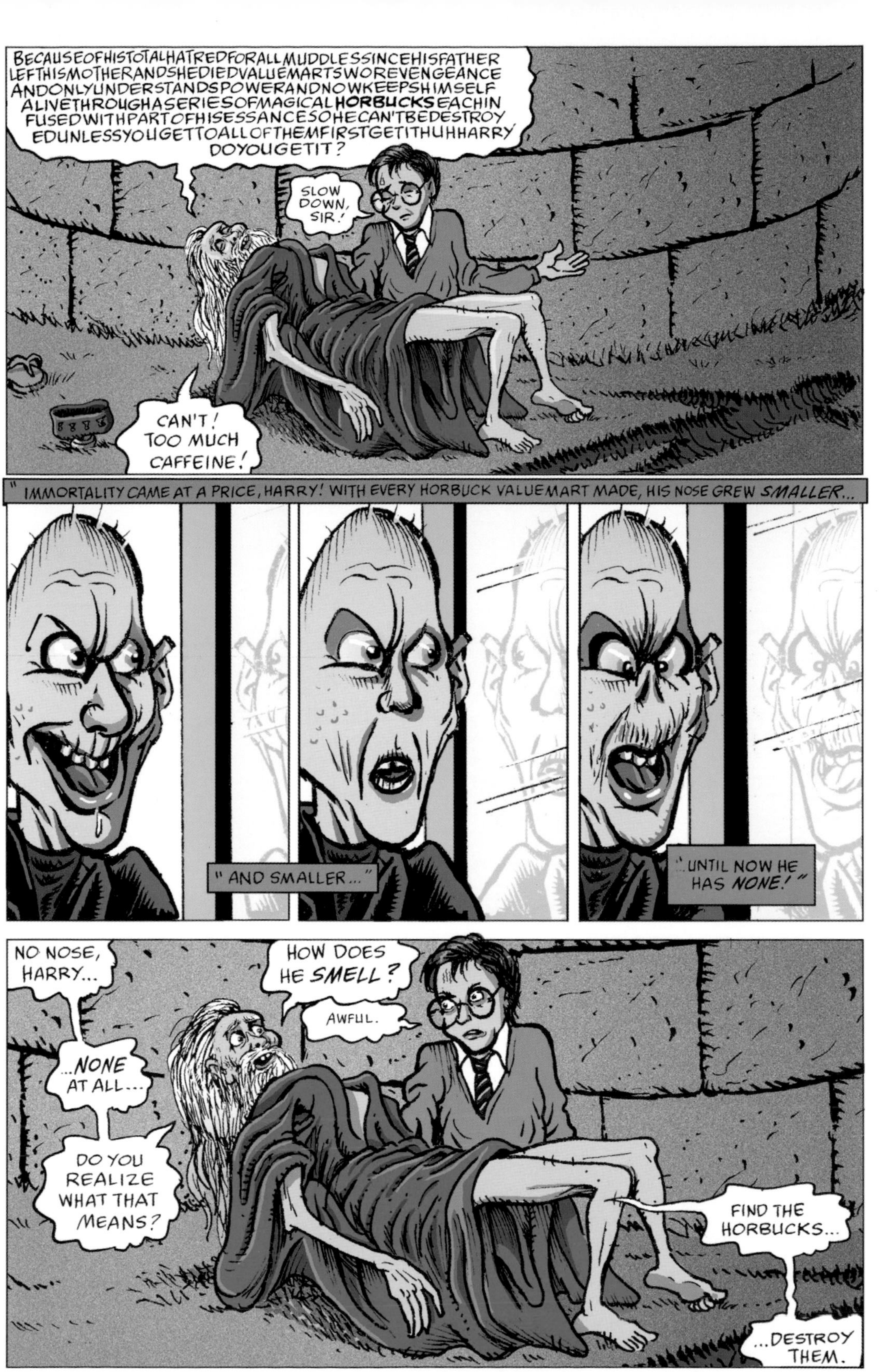
BECAUSEOFHISTOTALHATREDFORALLMUDDLESSINCEHISFATHER LEFTHISMOTHERANDSHEDIEDVALUEMARTSWOREVENGEANCE ANDONLYUNDERSTANDSPOWERANDNOWKEEPSHIMSELF ALIVETHROUGHASERIESOFMAGICAL**HORBUCKS**EACHIN FUSEDWITHPARTOFHISESSANCESOHECAN'TBEDESTROY EDUNLESSYOUGETTOALLOFTHEMFIRSTGETITHUHHARRY DOYOUGETIT?
SLOW DOWN, SIR!
CAN'T! TOO MUCH CAFFEINE!
"IMMORTALITY CAME AT A PRICE, HARRY! WITH EVERY HORBUCK VALUEMART MADE, HIS NOSE GREW *SMALLER*...
"AND SMALLER..."
"...UNTIL NOW HE HAS *NONE!*"
NO NOSE, HARRY...
HOW DOES HE *SMELL*?
AWFUL.
...*NONE* AT ALL...
DO YOU REALIZE WHAT THAT MEANS?
FIND THE HORBUCKS...
...DESTROY THEM.

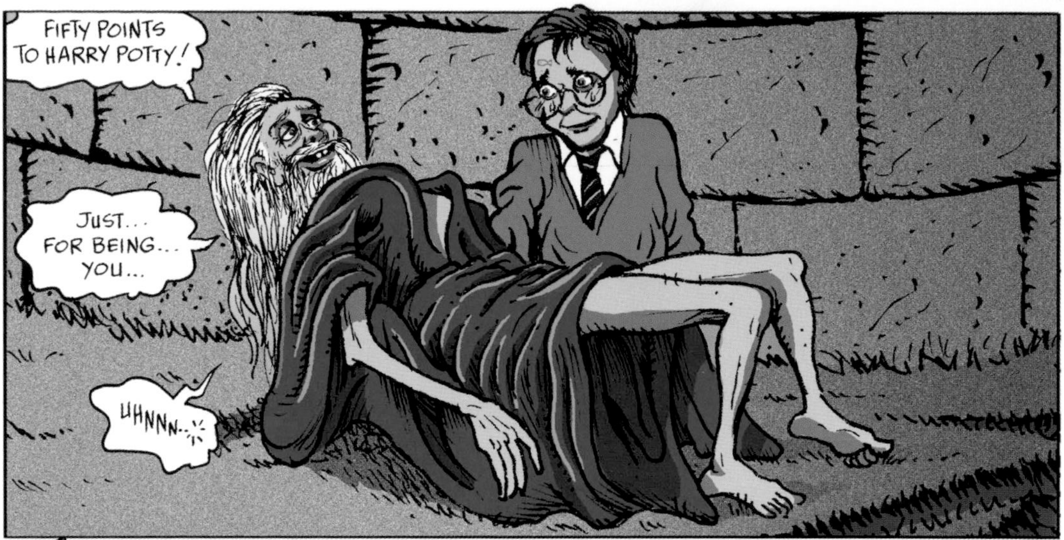
FIFTY POINTS TO HARRY POTTY!
JUST... FOR BEING... YOU...
UHNNN...

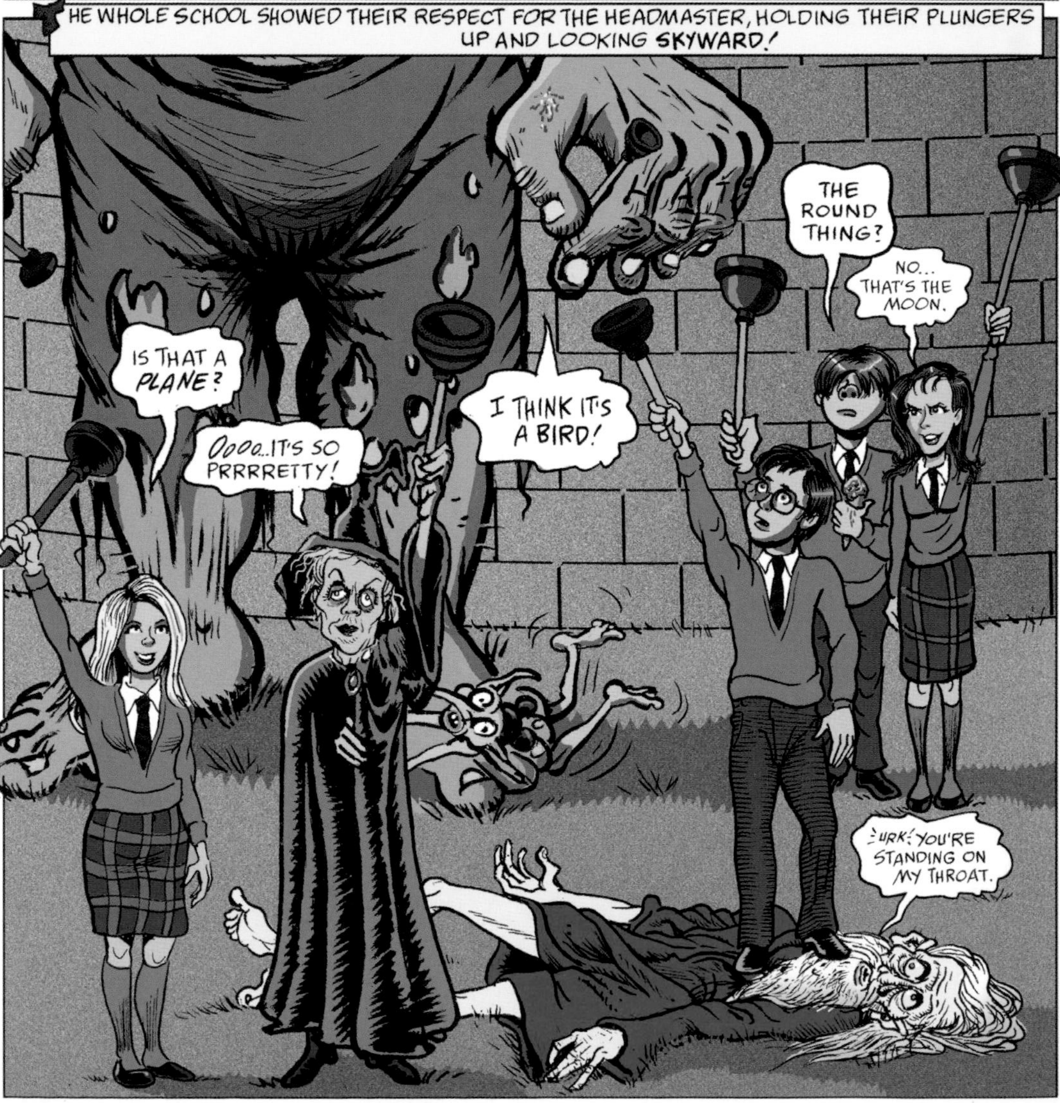
HE WHOLE SCHOOL SHOWED THEIR RESPECT FOR THE HEADMASTER, HOLDING THEIR PLUNGERS UP AND LOOKING SKYWARD!
IS THAT A PLANE?
OOOO...IT'S SO PRRRRETTY!
I THINK IT'S A BIRD!
THE ROUND THING?
NO... THAT'S THE MOON.
URK! YOU'RE STANDING ON MY THROAT.

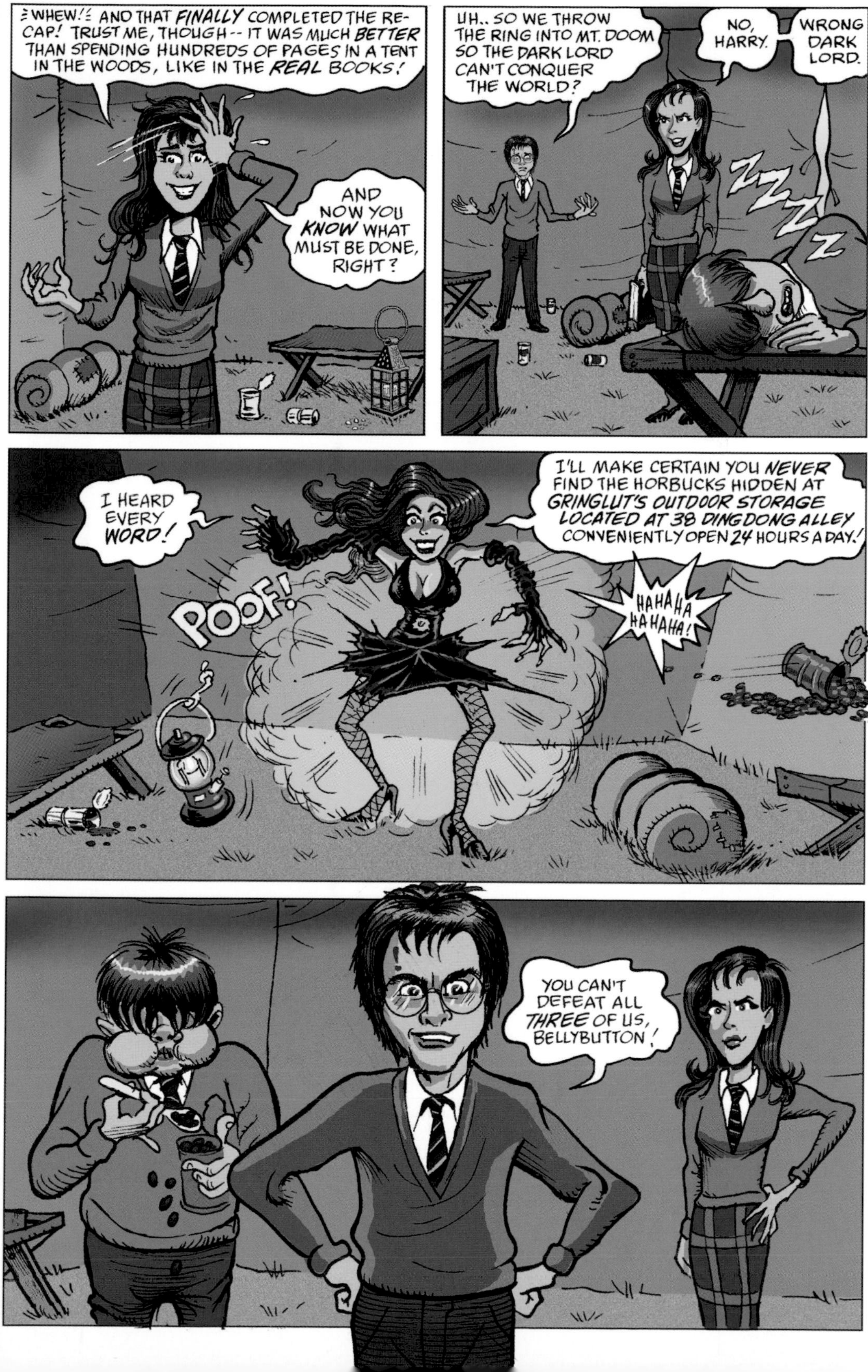

WHEW! AND THAT FINALLY COMPLETED THE RE-CAP! TRUST ME, THOUGH -- IT WAS MUCH BETTER THAN SPENDING HUNDREDS OF PAGES IN A TENT IN THE WOODS, LIKE IN THE REAL BOOKS!
AND NOW YOU KNOW WHAT MUST BE DONE, RIGHT?
UH.. SO WE THROW THE RING INTO MT. DOOM SO THE DARK LORD CAN'T CONQUER THE WORLD?
NO, HARRY.
WRONG DARK LORD.
I HEARD EVERY WORD!
I'LL MAKE CERTAIN YOU NEVER FIND THE HORBUCKS HIDDEN AT GRINGLUT'S OUTDOOR STORAGE LOCATED AT 38 DINGDONG ALLEY CONVENIENTLY OPEN 24 HOURS A DAY!
POOF!
HAHAHA HAHAHA!
YOU CAN'T DEFEAT ALL THREE OF US, BELLYBUTTON!

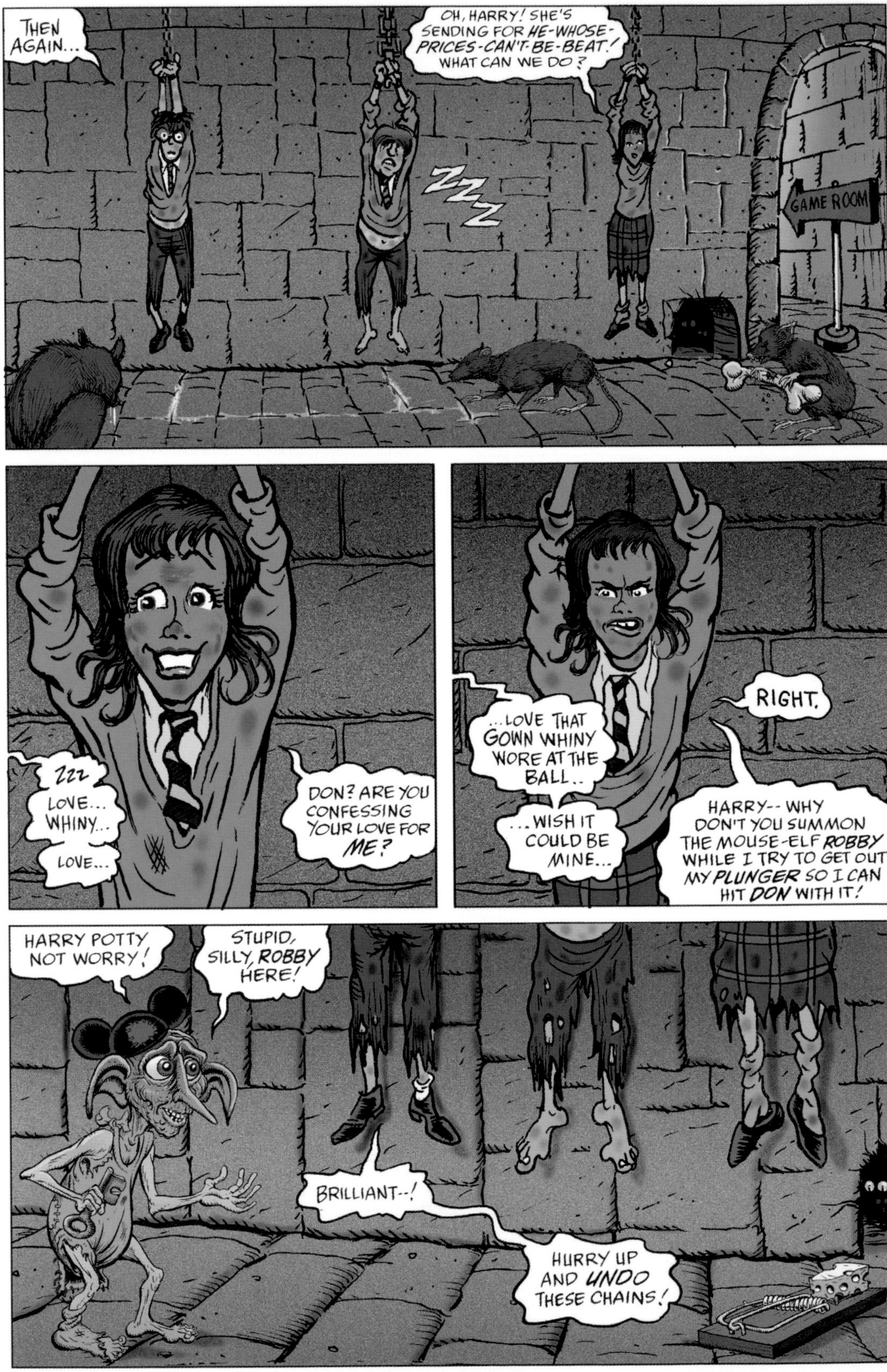
THEN AGAIN...
OH, HARRY! SHE'S SENDING FOR HE-WHOSE-PRICES-CAN'T-BE-BEAT! WHAT CAN WE DO?
ZZZ
GAME ROOM
ZZZ LOVE... WHINY... LOVE...
DON? ARE YOU CONFESSING YOUR LOVE FOR ME?
...LOVE THAT GOWN WHINY WORE AT THE BALL..
...WISH IT COULD BE MINE...
RIGHT.
HARRY-- WHY DON'T YOU SUMMON THE MOUSE-ELF ROBBY WHILE I TRY TO GET OUT MY PLUNGER SO I CAN HIT DON WITH IT!
HARRY POTTY NOT WORRY!
STUPID, SILLY, ROBBY HERE!
BRILLIANT--!
HURRY UP AND UNDO THESE CHAINS!

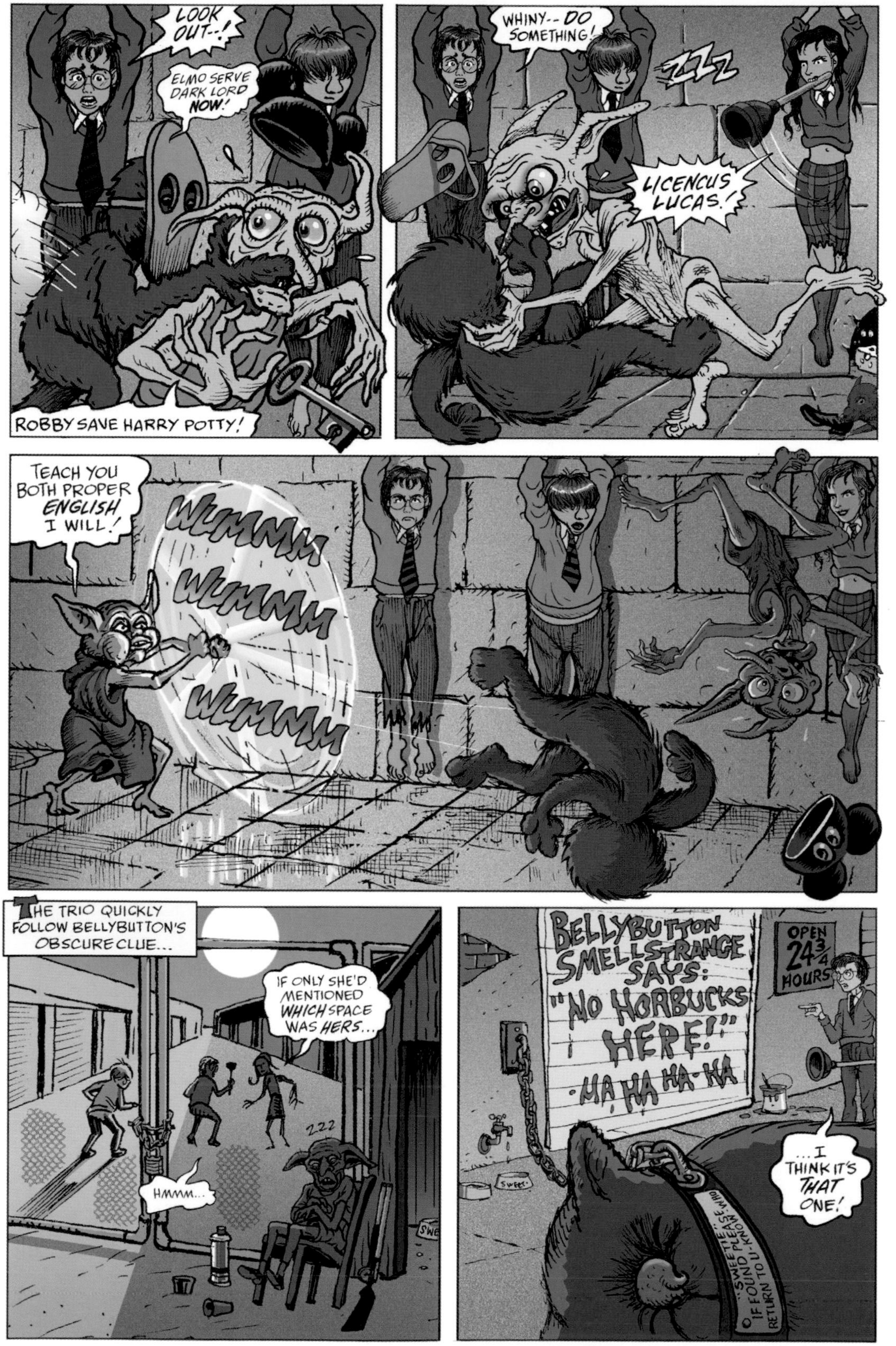
LOOK OUT--!
ELMO SERVE DARK LORD NOW!
ROBBY SAVE HARRY POTTY!
WHINY-- DO SOMETHING!
ZZZ
LICENCUS LUCAS!
TEACH YOU BOTH PROPER ENGLISH I WILL!
WUMMM
WUMMMM
WUMMMM
THE TRIO QUICKLY FOLLOW BELLYBUTTON'S OBSCURE CLUE...
IF ONLY SHE'D MENTIONED WHICH SPACE WAS HERS...
ZZZ
HMMM...
SWE
BELLYBUTTON SMELLSTRANGE SAYS: "NO HORBUCKS HERE!" HA HA HA HA
OPEN 24 3/4 HOURS
SWEET
...I THINK IT'S THAT ONE!
"SWEETIE" IF FOUND PLEASE RETURN TO U-KNOW-WHO

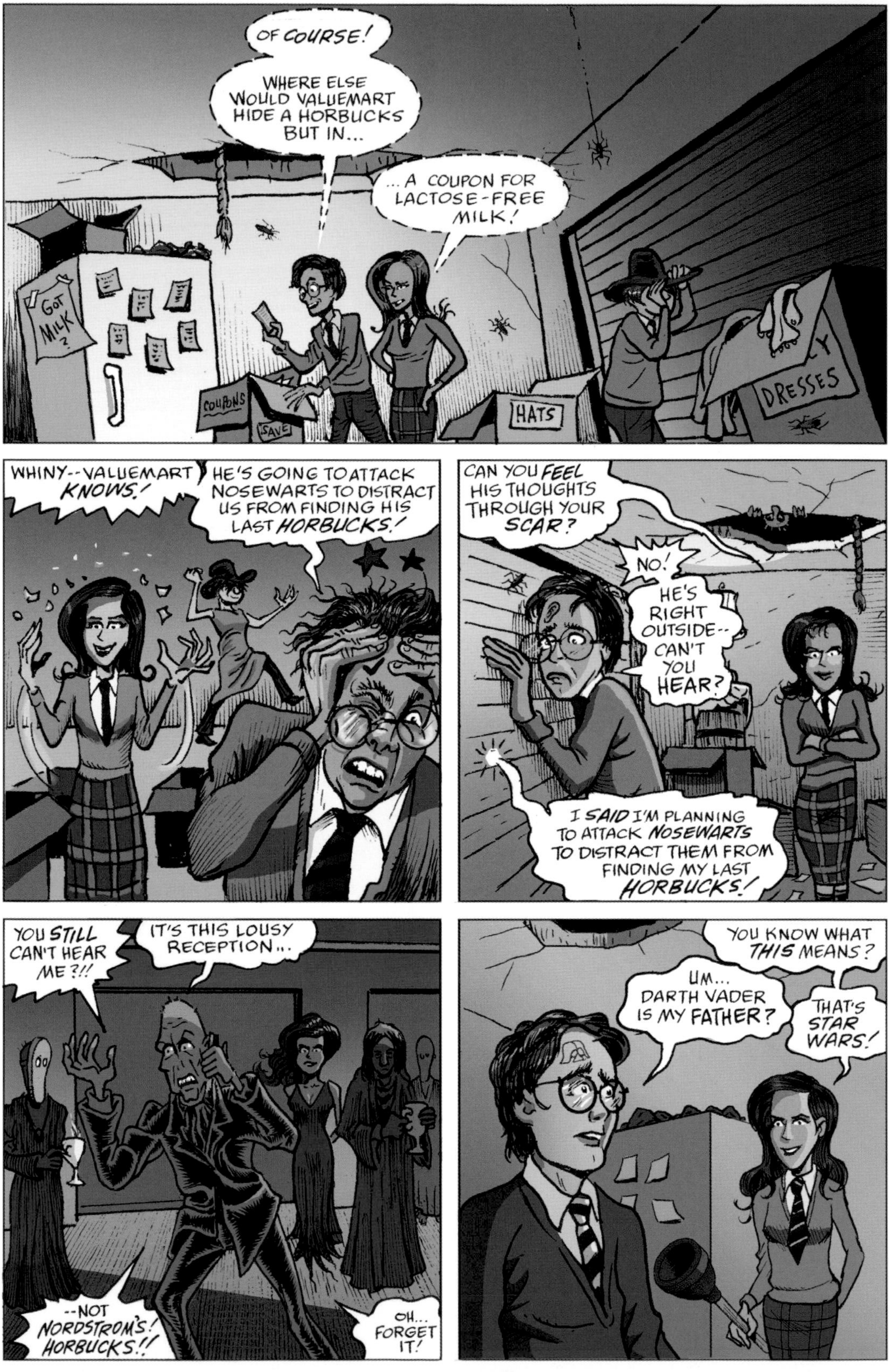
OF COURSE!
WHERE ELSE WOULD VALUEMART HIDE A HORBUCKS BUT IN...
...A COUPON FOR LACTOSE-FREE MILK!
GOT MILK ?
COUPONS
SAVE
HATS
DRESSES
WHINY--VALUEMART KNOWS!
HE'S GOING TO ATTACK NOSEWARTS TO DISTRACT US FROM FINDING HIS LAST HORBUCKS!
CAN YOU FEEL HIS THOUGHTS THROUGH YOUR SCAR?
NO!
HE'S RIGHT OUTSIDE-- CAN'T YOU HEAR?
I SAID I'M PLANNING TO ATTACK NOSEWARTS TO DISTRACT THEM FROM FINDING MY LAST HORBUCKS!
YOU STILL CAN'T HEAR ME?!!
IT'S THIS LOUSY RECEPTION...
--NOT NORDSTROM'S! HORBUCKS!!
OH... FORGET IT!
YOU KNOW WHAT THIS MEANS?
UM... DARTH VADER IS MY FATHER?
THAT'S STAR WARS!

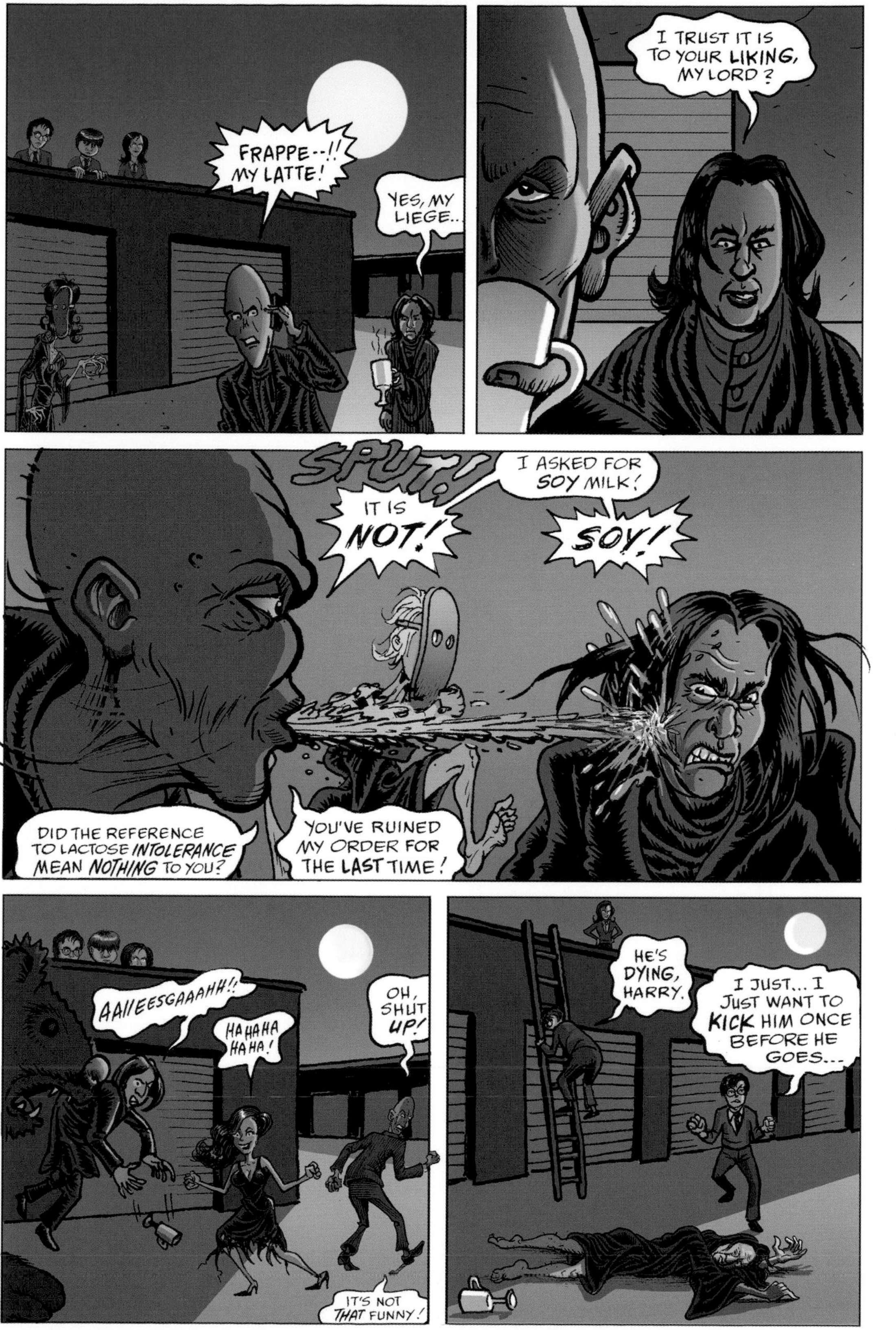

FRAPPE--!! MY LATTE!
YES, MY LIEGE..
I TRUST IT IS TO YOUR LIKING, MY LORD?
SPUT!
IT IS NOT!
I ASKED FOR SOY MILK!
SOY!
DID THE REFERENCE TO LACTOSE INTOLERANCE MEAN NOTHING TO YOU?
YOU'VE RUINED MY ORDER FOR THE LAST TIME!
AAIIEESGAAAHH!!
HAHAHA HAHA!
OH, SHUT UP!
IT'S NOT THAT FUNNY!
HE'S DYING, HARRY.
I JUST... I JUST WANT TO KICK HIM ONCE BEFORE HE GOES...

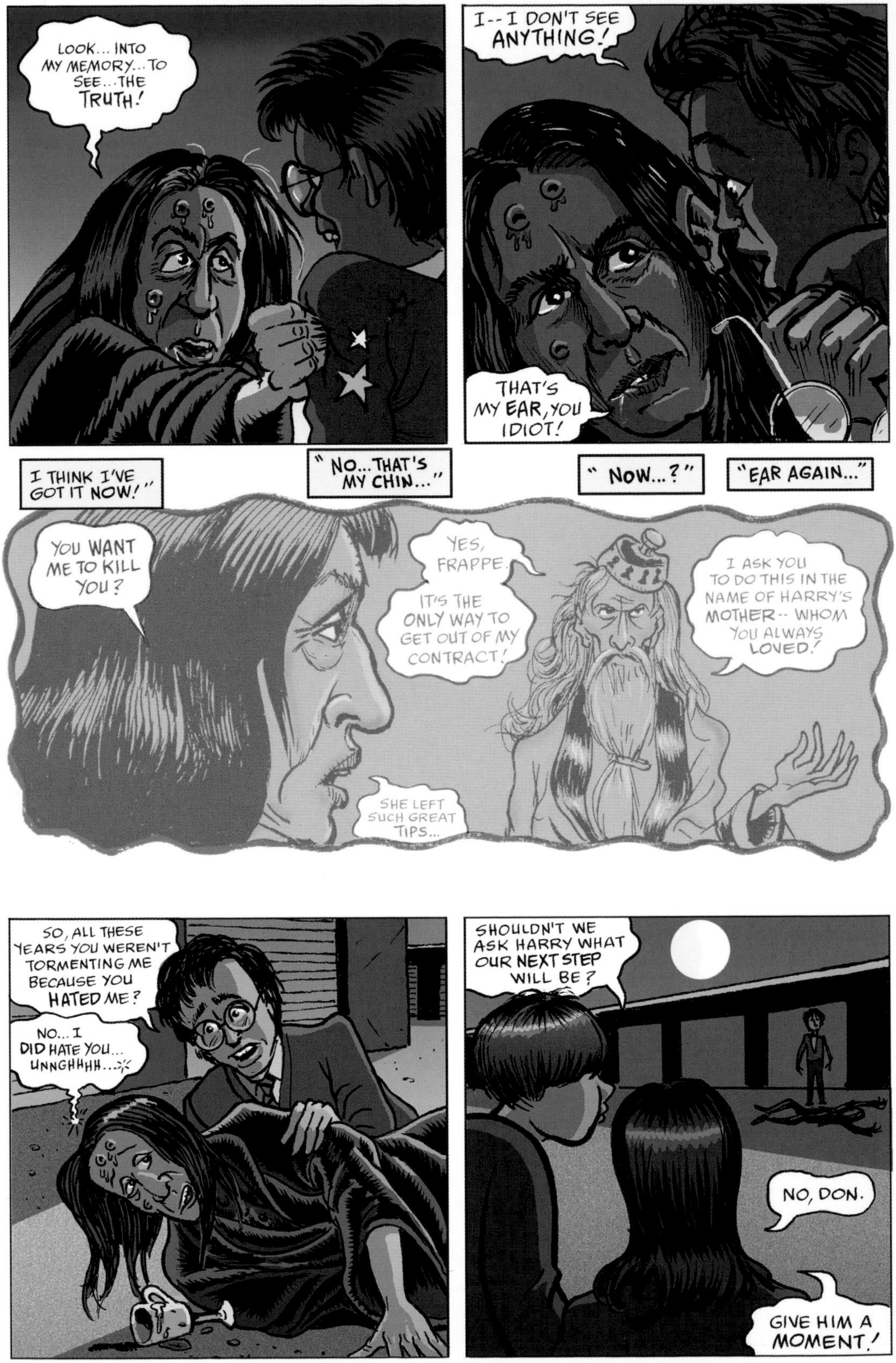
LOOK... INTO MY MEMORY... TO SEE... THE TRUTH!
I-- I DON'T SEE ANYTHING!
THAT'S MY EAR, YOU IDIOT!
"I THINK I'VE GOT IT NOW!"
"NO... THAT'S MY CHIN..."
"NOW...?"
"EAR AGAIN..."
YOU WANT ME TO KILL YOU?
YES, FRAPPE.
IT'S THE ONLY WAY TO GET OUT OF MY CONTRACT!
I ASK YOU TO DO THIS IN THE NAME OF HARRY'S MOTHER-- WHOM YOU ALWAYS LOVED!
SHE LEFT SUCH GREAT TIPS...
SO, ALL THESE YEARS YOU WEREN'T TORMENTING ME BECAUSE YOU HATED ME?
NO... I DID HATE YOU... UNNGHHHH...
SHOULDN'T WE ASK HARRY WHAT OUR NEXT STEP WILL BE?
NO, DON.
GIVE HIM A MOMENT!

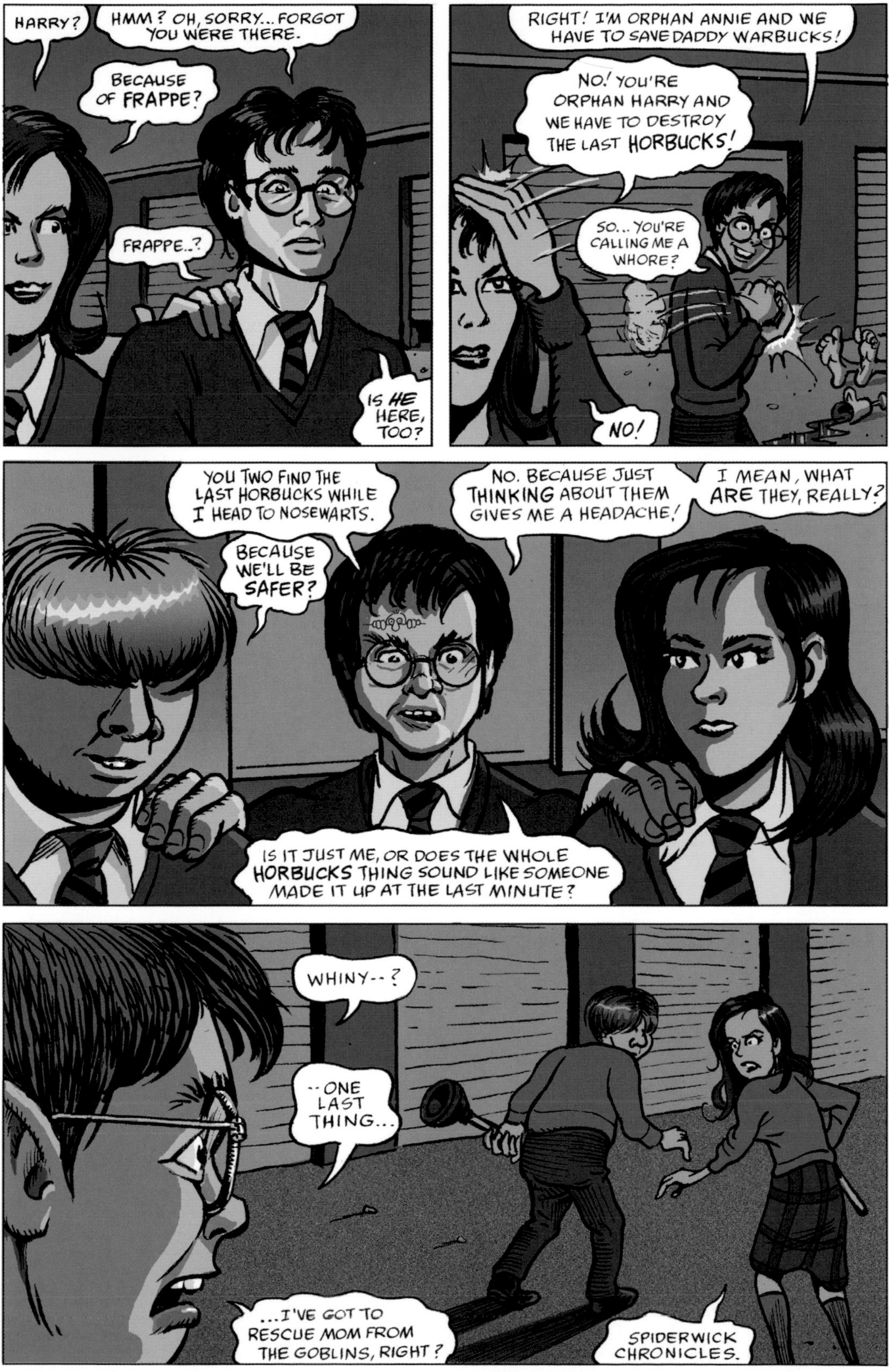
HARRY?
HMM? OH, SORRY... FORGOT YOU WERE THERE.
BECAUSE OF FRAPPE?
FRAPPE..?
IS HE HERE, TOO?
RIGHT! I'M ORPHAN ANNIE AND WE HAVE TO SAVE DADDY WARBUCKS!
NO! YOU'RE ORPHAN HARRY AND WE HAVE TO DESTROY THE LAST HORBUCKS!
SO... YOU'RE CALLING ME A WHORE?
NO!
YOU TWO FIND THE LAST HORBUCKS WHILE I HEAD TO NOSEWARTS.
BECAUSE WE'LL BE SAFER?
NO. BECAUSE JUST THINKING ABOUT THEM GIVES ME A HEADACHE!
I MEAN, WHAT ARE THEY, REALLY?
IS IT JUST ME, OR DOES THE WHOLE HORBUCKS THING SOUND LIKE SOMEONE MADE IT UP AT THE LAST MINUTE?
WHINY--?
--ONE LAST THING...
...I'VE GOT TO RESCUE MOM FROM THE GOBLINS, RIGHT?
SPIDERWICK CHRONICLES.

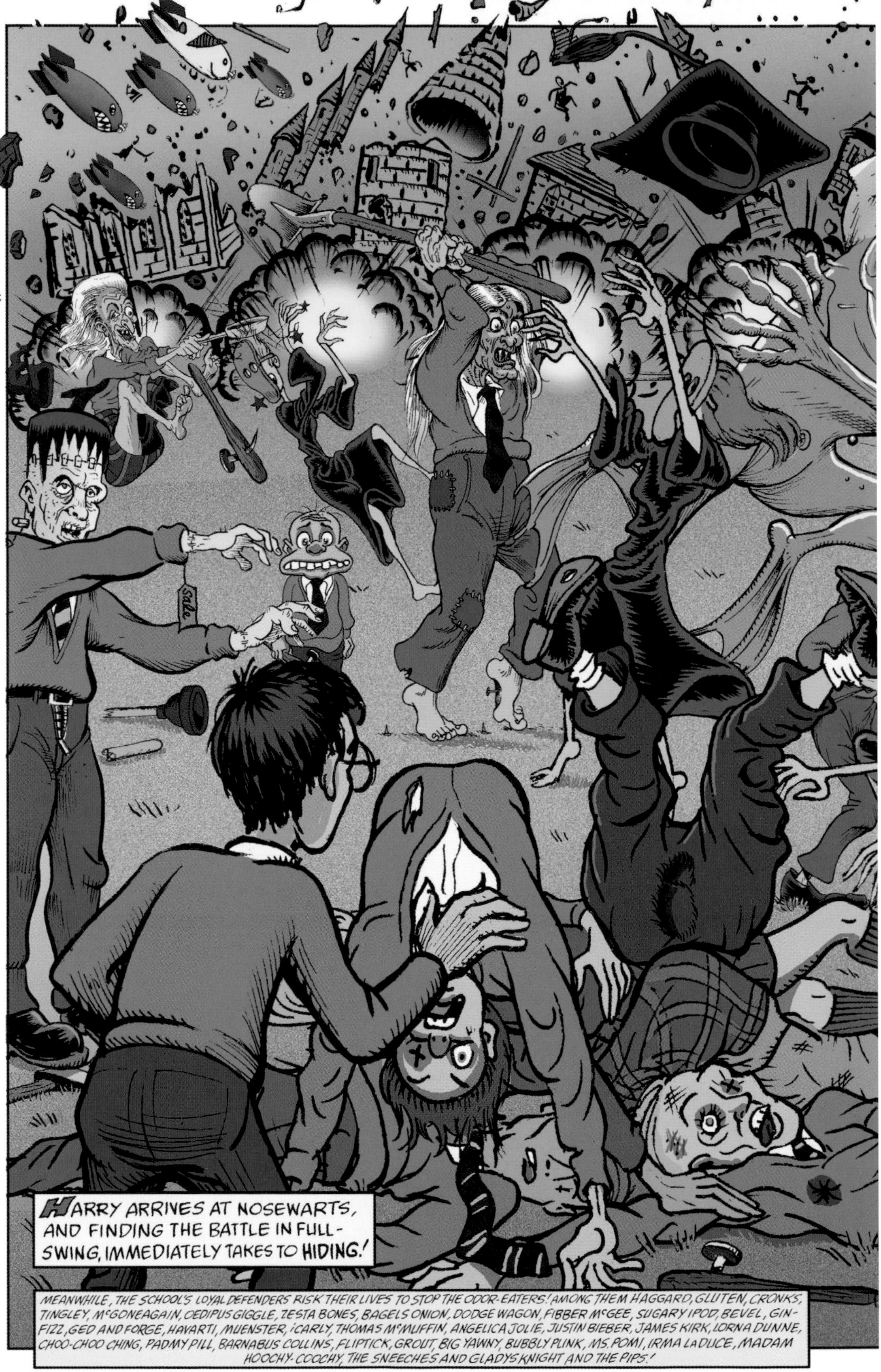
HARRY ARRIVES AT NOSEWARTS, AND FINDING THE BATTLE IN FULL-SWING, IMMEDIATELY TAKES TO HIDING!
MEANWHILE, THE SCHOOL'S LOYAL DEFENDERS RISK THEIR LIVES TO STOP THE ODOR-EATERS! AMONG THEM HAGGARD, GLUTEN, CRONKS, TINGLEY, McGONEAGAIN, OEDIPUS GIGGLE, ZESTA BONES, BAGELS ONION, DODGE WAGON, FIBBER McGEE, SUGARY IPOD, BEVEL, GIN-FIZZ, GED AND FORGE, HAVARTI, MUENSTER, iCARLY, THOMAS McMUFFIN, ANGELICA JOLIE, JUSTIN BIEBER, JAMES KIRK, LORNA DUNNE, CHOO-CHOO CHING, PADMY PILL, BARNABUS COLLINS, FLIPTICK, GROUT, BIG YAWNY, BUBBLY PLINK, MS. POMI, IRMA LaDUCE, MADAM HOOCHY-COOCHY, THE SNEECHES AND GLADYS KNIGHT AND THE PIPS!
Sale

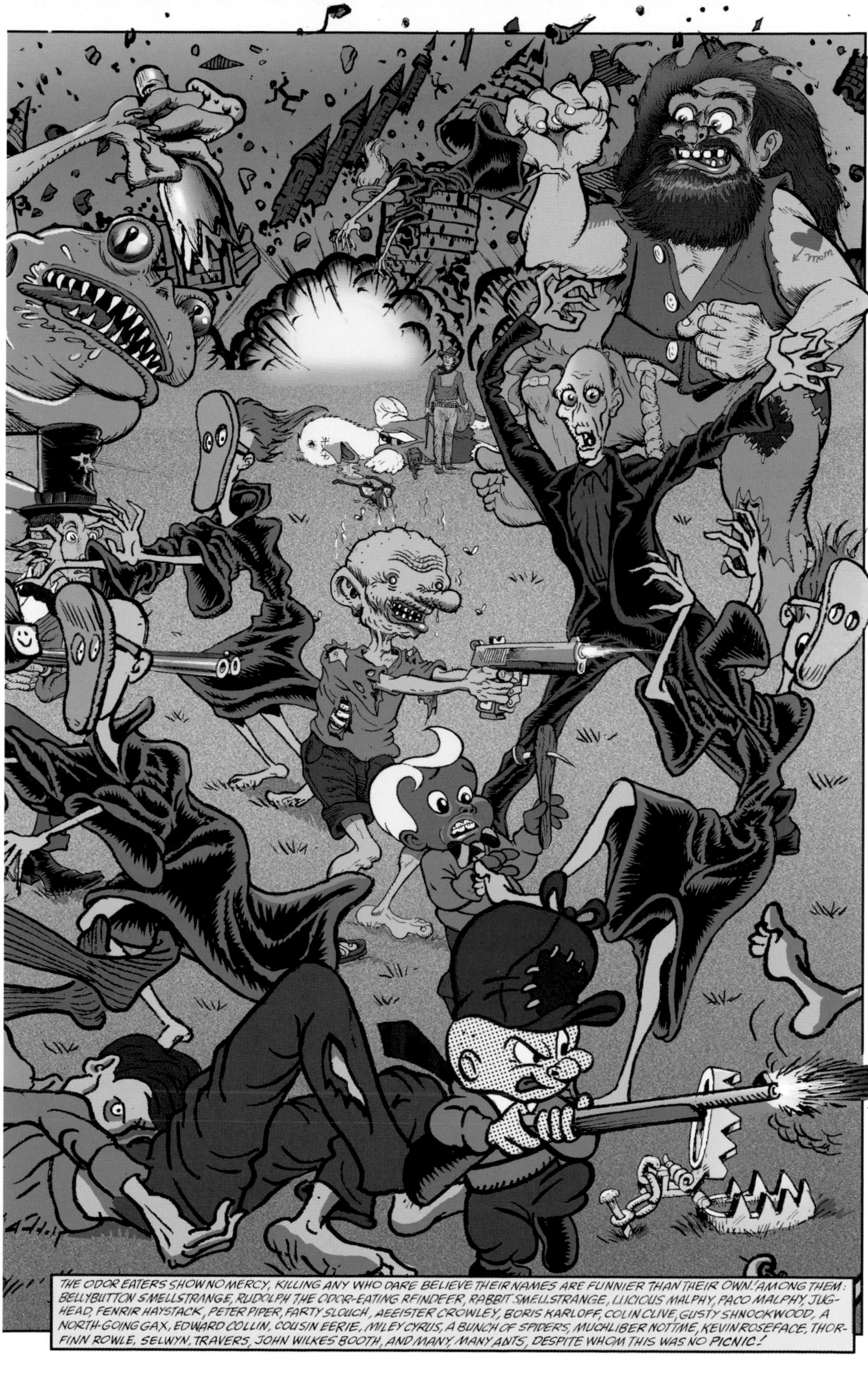
MOM
THE ODOR EATERS SHOW NO MERCY, KILLING ANY WHO DARE BELIEVE THEIR NAMES ARE FUNNIER THAN THEIR OWN! AMONG THEM: BELLYBUTTON SMELLSTRANGE, RUDOLPH THE ODOR-EATING REINDEER, RABBIT SMELLSTRANGE, LUCIOUS MALPHY, PACO MALPHY, JUGHEAD, FENRIR HAYSTACK, PETER PIPER, FARTY SLOUCH, AEEISTER CROWLEY, BORIS KARLOFF, COLIN CLIVE, GUSTY SHNOOKWOOD, A NORTH-GOING GAX, EDWARD COLLIN, COUSIN EERIE, MILEY CYRUS, A BUNCH OF SPIDERS, MUCHLIBER NOTTME, KEVIN ROSEFACE, THORFINN ROWLE, SELWYN, TRAVERS, JOHN WILKES BOOTH, AND MANY, MANY ANTS, DESPITE WHOM THIS WAS NO PICNIC!

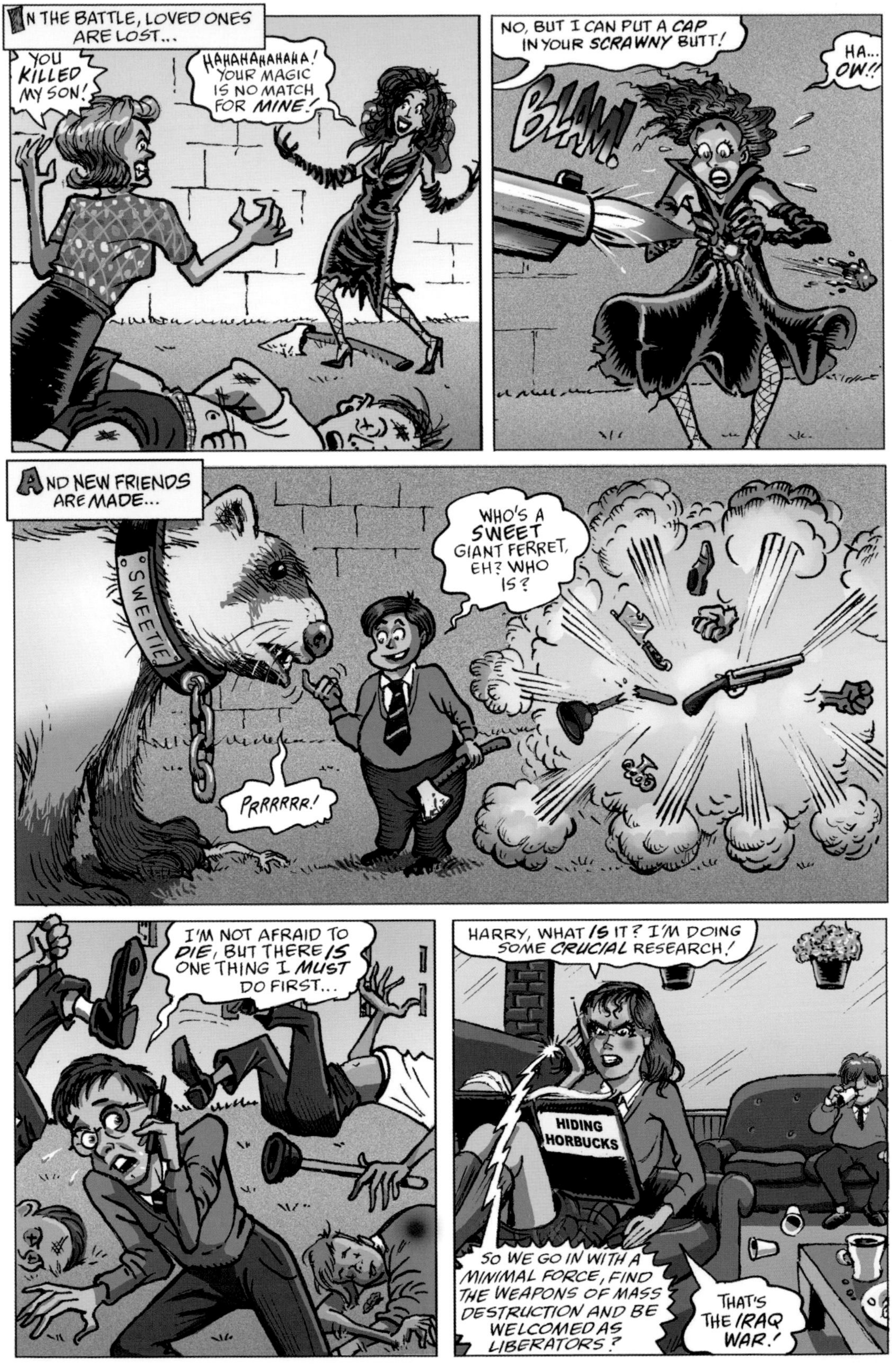
IN THE BATTLE, LOVED ONES ARE LOST...
YOU KILLED MY SON!
HAHAHAHAHAHA! YOUR MAGIC IS NO MATCH FOR MINE!
NO, BUT I CAN PUT A CAP IN YOUR SCRAWNY BUTT!
BLAM!
HA... OW!!
AND NEW FRIENDS ARE MADE...
SWEETIE
WHO'S A SWEET GIANT FERRET, EH? WHO IS?
PRRRRRR!
I'M NOT AFRAID TO DIE, BUT THERE IS ONE THING I MUST DO FIRST...
HARRY, WHAT IS IT? I'M DOING SOME CRUCIAL RESEARCH!
HIDING HORBUCKS
SO WE GO IN WITH A MINIMAL FORCE, FIND THE WEAPONS OF MASS DESTRUCTION AND BE WELCOMED AS LIBERATORS?
THAT'S THE IRAQ WAR!

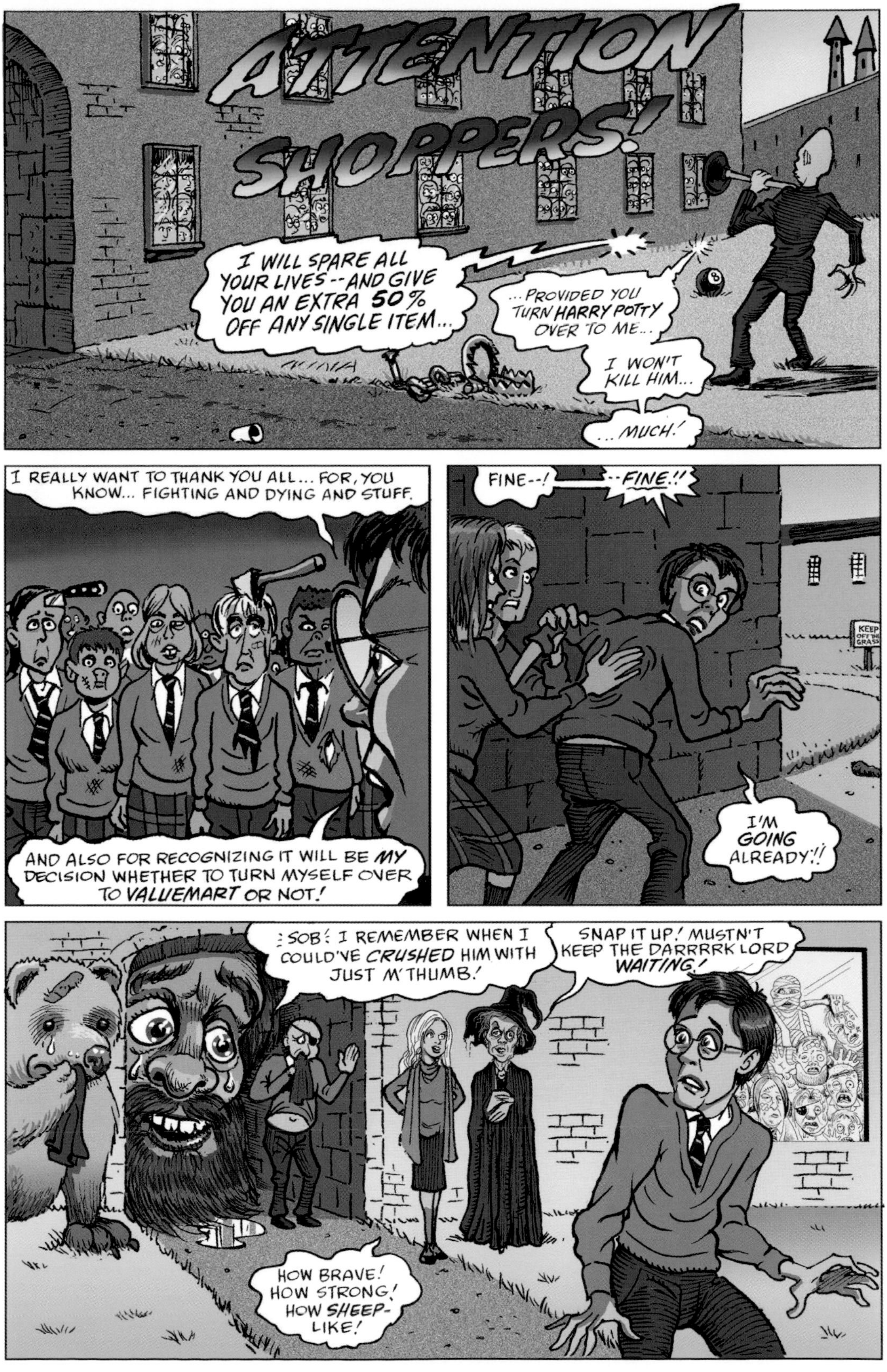
ATTENTION SHOPPERS!
I WILL SPARE ALL YOUR LIVES--AND GIVE YOU AN EXTRA 50% OFF ANY SINGLE ITEM...
...PROVIDED YOU TURN HARRY POTTY OVER TO ME...
I WON'T KILL HIM...
...MUCH!
I REALLY WANT TO THANK YOU ALL... FOR, YOU KNOW... FIGHTING AND DYING AND STUFF.
AND ALSO FOR RECOGNIZING IT WILL BE MY DECISION WHETHER TO TURN MYSELF OVER TO VALUEMART OR NOT!
FINE--!
--FINE!!
KEEP OFF THE GRASS
I'M GOING ALREADY!!
:SOB: I REMEMBER WHEN I COULD'VE CRUSHED HIM WITH JUST M'THUMB!
SNAP IT UP! MUSTN'T KEEP THE DARRRRK LORD WAITING!
HOW BRAVE! HOW STRONG! HOW SHEEP-LIKE!

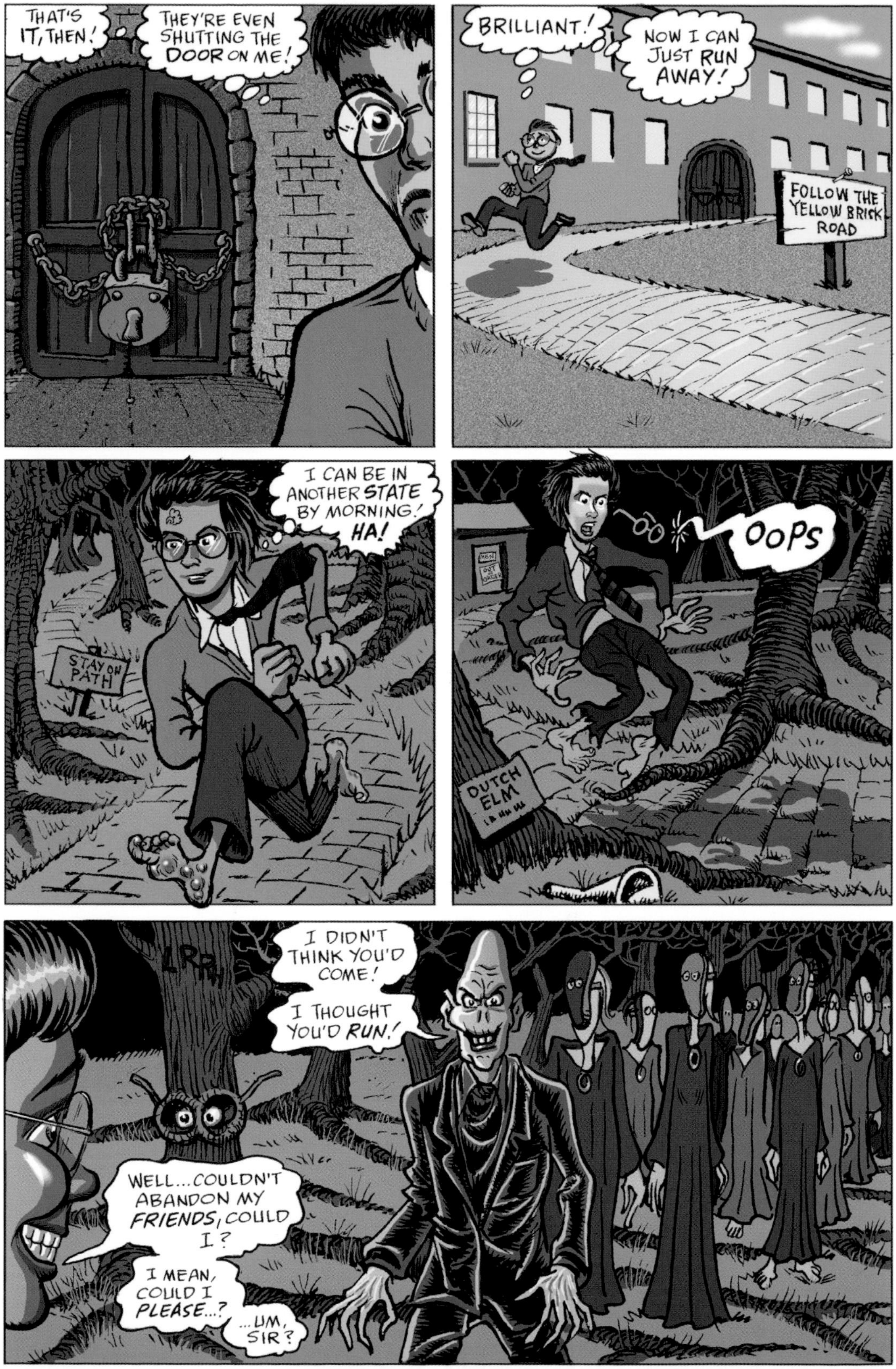
THAT'S IT, THEN!
THEY'RE EVEN SHUTTING THE DOOR ON ME!
BRILLIANT!
NOW I CAN JUST RUN AWAY!
FOLLOW THE YELLOW BRICK ROAD
I CAN BE IN ANOTHER STATE BY MORNING! HA!
STAY ON PATH
OOPS
DUTCH ELM
I DIDN'T THINK YOU'D COME!
I THOUGHT YOU'D RUN!
WELL... COULDN'T ABANDON MY FRIENDS, COULD I?
I MEAN, COULD I PLEASE...?
...UM, SIR?

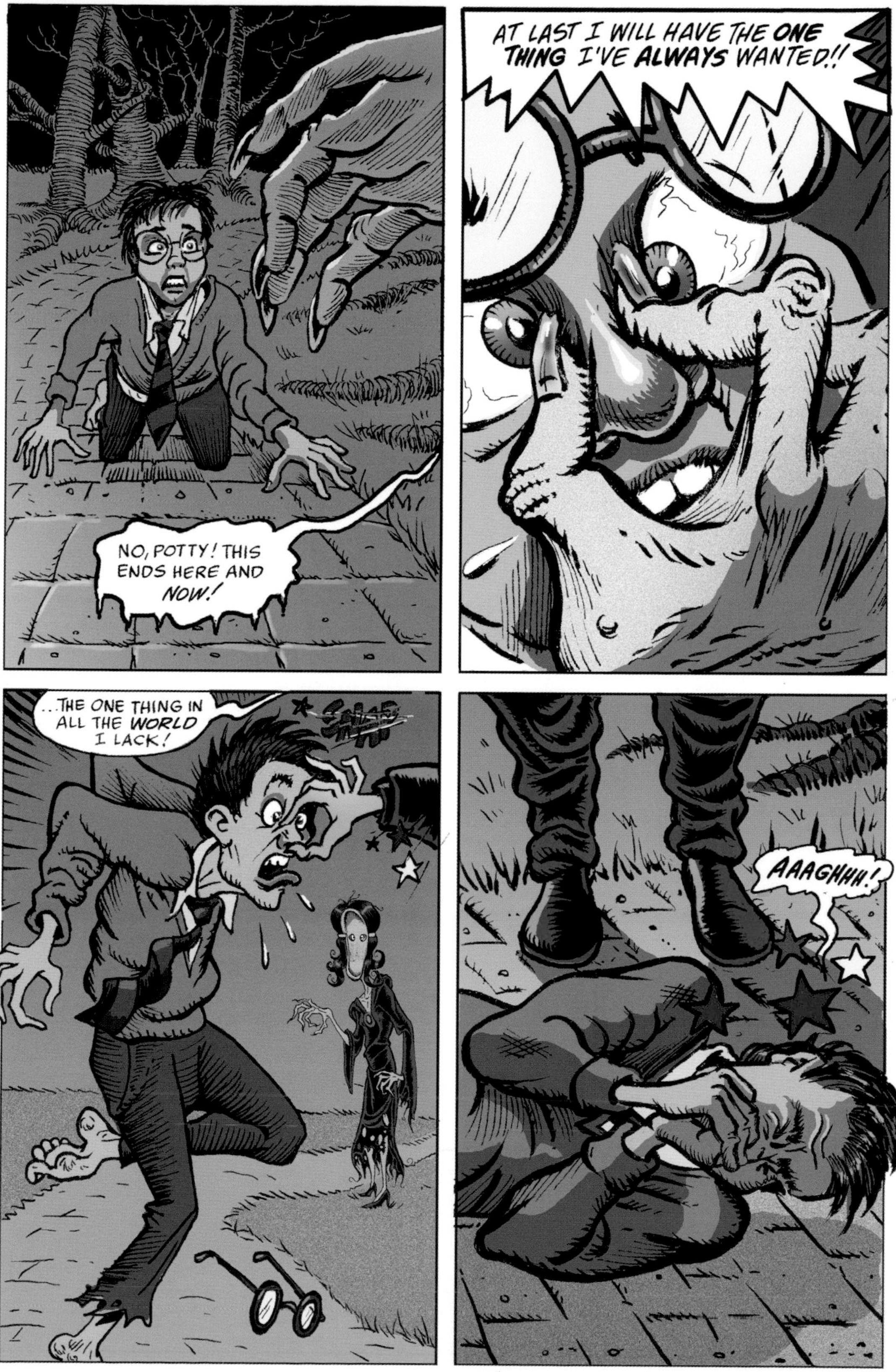
NO, POTTY! THIS ENDS HERE AND NOW!
AT LAST I WILL HAVE THE ONE THING I'VE ALWAYS WANTED!!
...THE ONE THING IN ALL THE WORLD I LACK!
AAAGHHH!

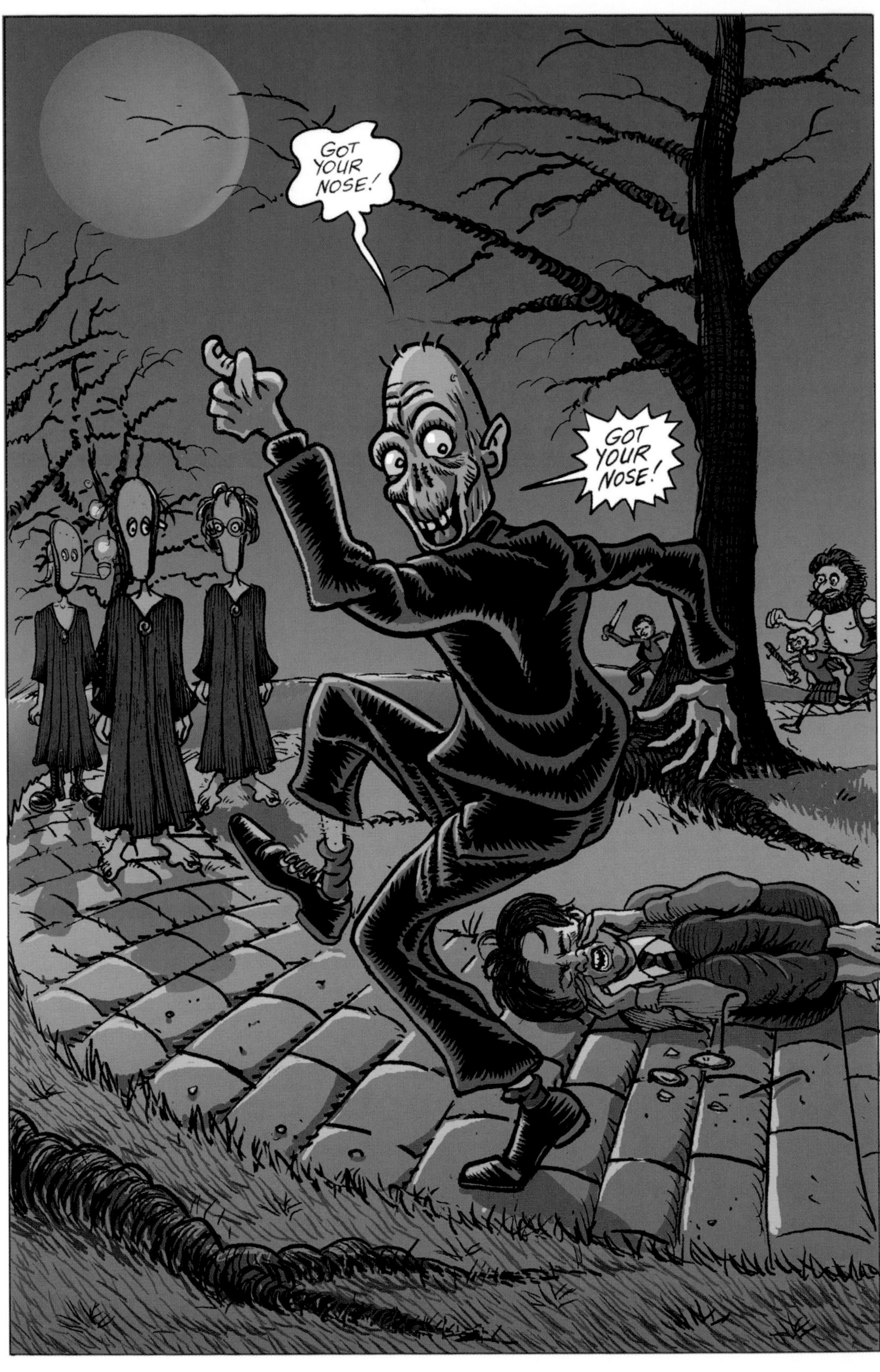
GOT YOUR NOSE!
GOT YOUR NOSE!

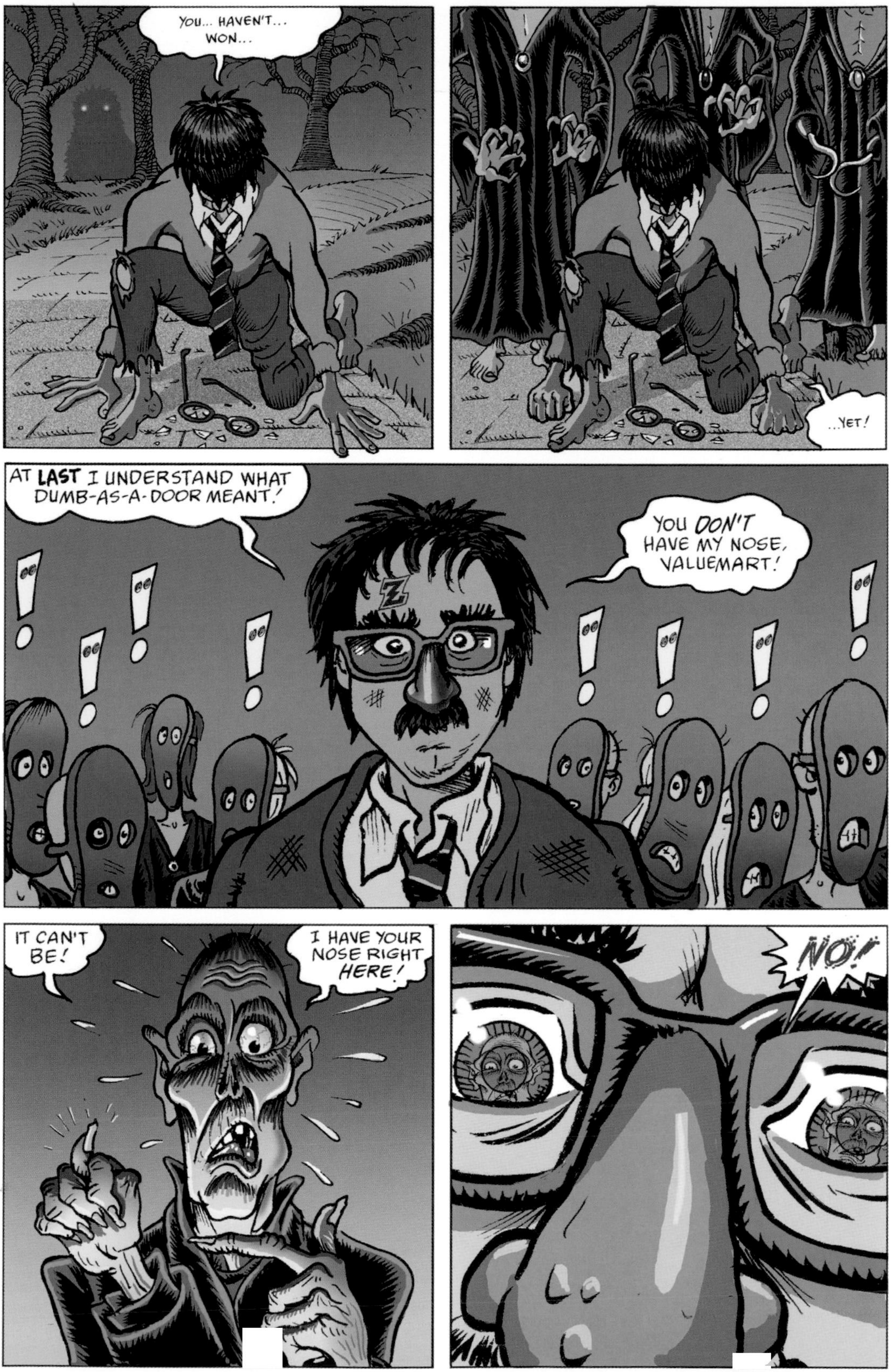

YOU... HAVEN'T... WON...
...YET!
AT LAST I UNDERSTAND WHAT DUMB-AS-A-DOOR MEANT!
YOU DON'T HAVE MY NOSE, VALUEMART!
IT CAN'T BE!
I HAVE YOUR NOSE RIGHT HERE!
NO!

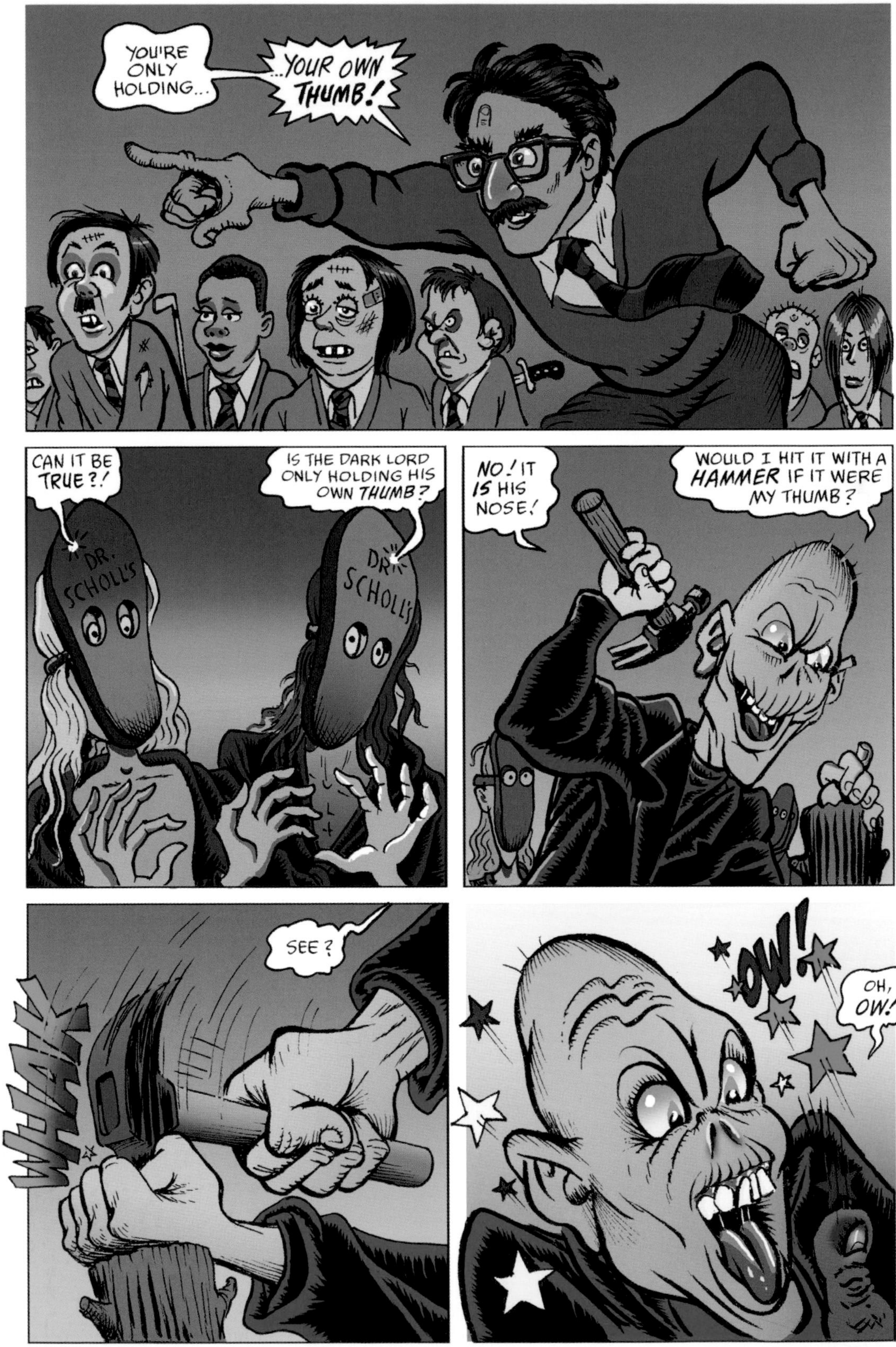
YOU'RE ONLY HOLDING...
...YOUR OWN THUMB!
CAN IT BE TRUE?!
IS THE DARK LORD ONLY HOLDING HIS OWN THUMB?
DR. SCHOLL'S
DR. SCHOLL'S
NO! IT IS HIS NOSE!
WOULD I HIT IT WITH A HAMMER IF IT WERE MY THUMB?
SEE?
WHAK
OW!
OH, OW!

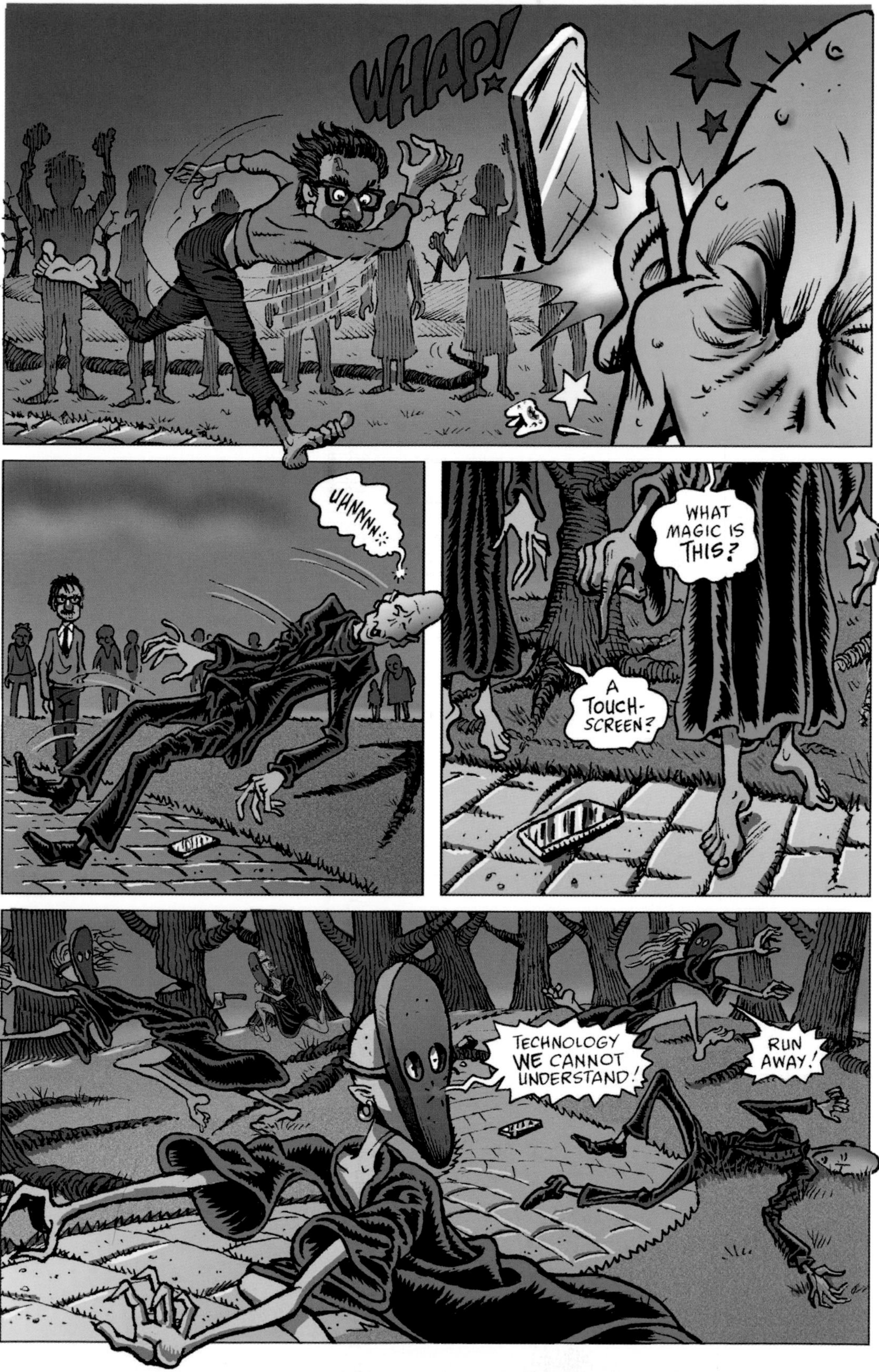
WHAP!
UHNNN...
WHAT MAGIC IS THIS?
A TOUCH-SCREEN?
TECHNOLOGY WE CANNOT UNDERSTAND!
RUN AWAY!

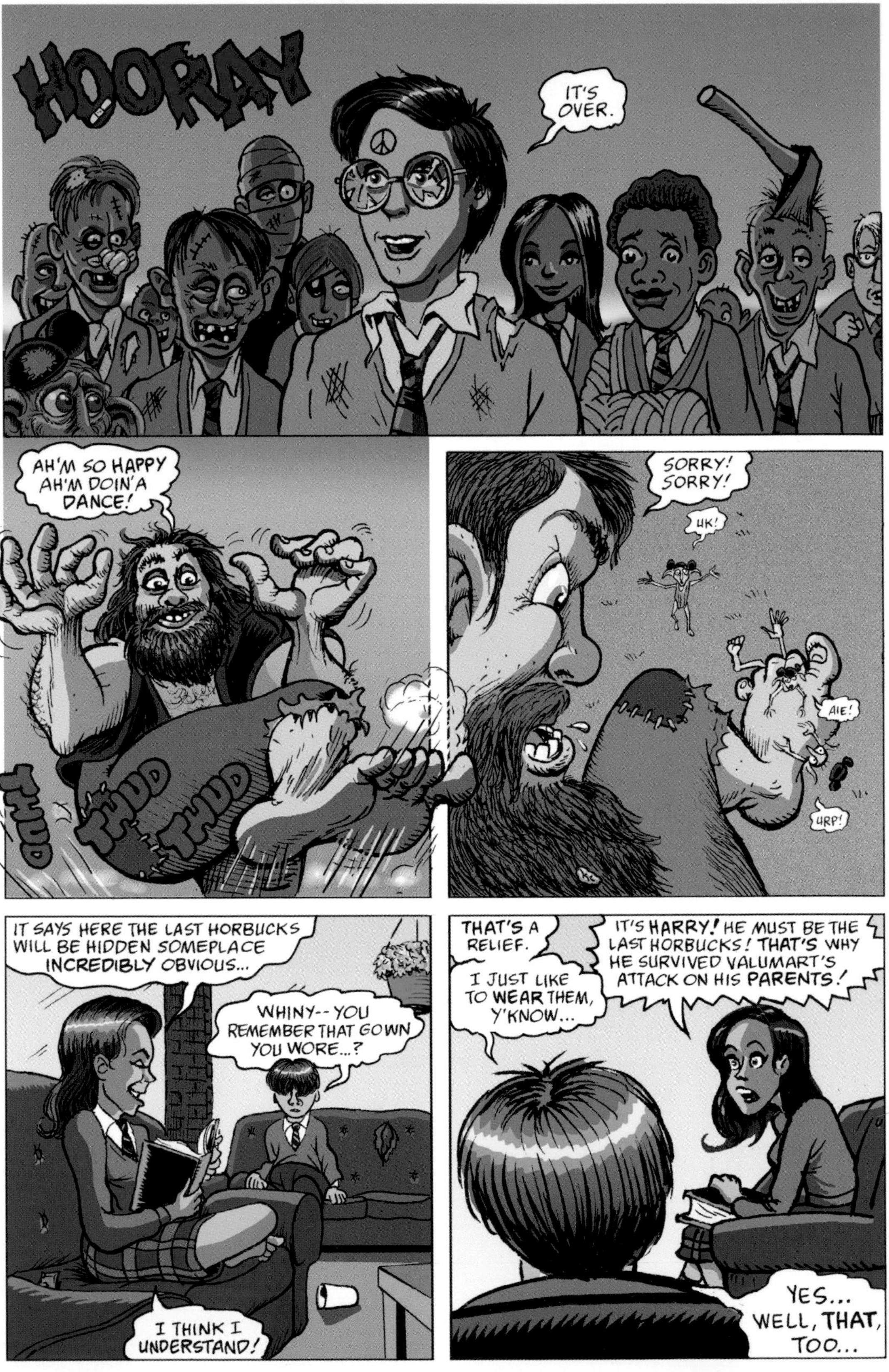
HOORAY
IT'S OVER.
AH'M SO HAPPY AH'M DOIN'A DANCE!
THUD THUD THUD
SORRY! SORRY!
UK!
AIE!
URP!
IT SAYS HERE THE LAST HORBUCKS WILL BE HIDDEN SOMEPLACE INCREDIBLY OBVIOUS...
WHINY-- YOU REMEMBER THAT GOWN YOU WORE...?
I THINK I UNDERSTAND!
THAT'S A RELIEF.
I JUST LIKE TO WEAR THEM, Y'KNOW...
IT'S HARRY! HE MUST BE THE LAST HORBUCKS! THAT'S WHY HE SURVIVED VALUMART'S ATTACK ON HIS PARENTS!
YES... WELL, THAT, TOO...

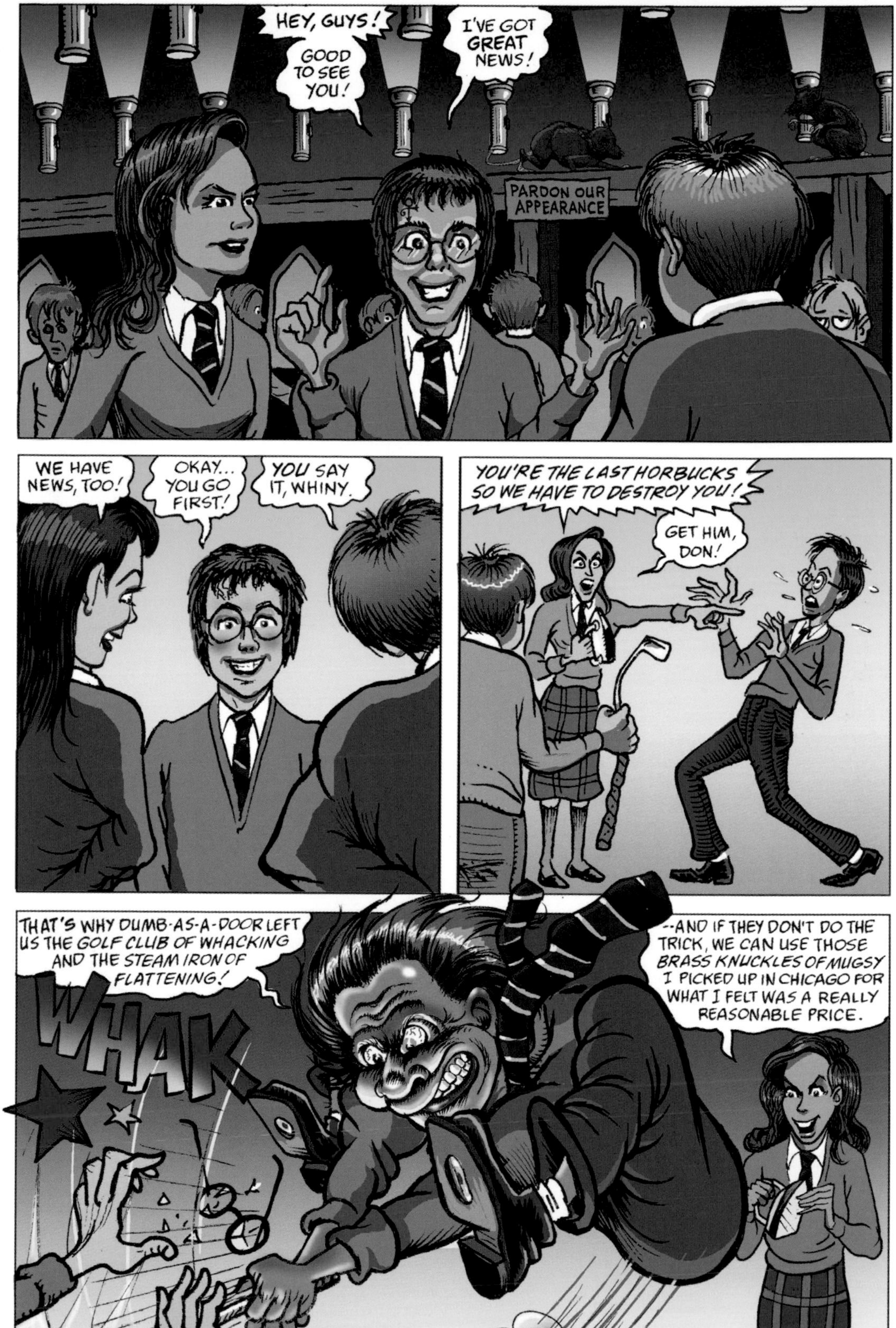

HEY, GUYS!
GOOD TO SEE YOU!
I'VE GOT GREAT NEWS!
PARDON OUR APPEARANCE
WE HAVE NEWS, TOO!
OKAY... YOU GO FIRST!
YOU SAY IT, WHINY.
YOU'RE THE LAST HORBUCKS SO WE HAVE TO DESTROY YOU!
GET HIM, DON!
THAT'S WHY DUMB-AS-A-DOOR LEFT US THE GOLF CLUB OF WHACKING AND THE STEAM IRON OF FLATTENING!
WHAK
--AND IF THEY DON'T DO THE TRICK, WE CAN USE THOSE BRASS KNUCKLES OF MUGSY I PICKED UP IN CHICAGO FOR WHAT I FELT WAS A REALLY REASONABLE PRICE.

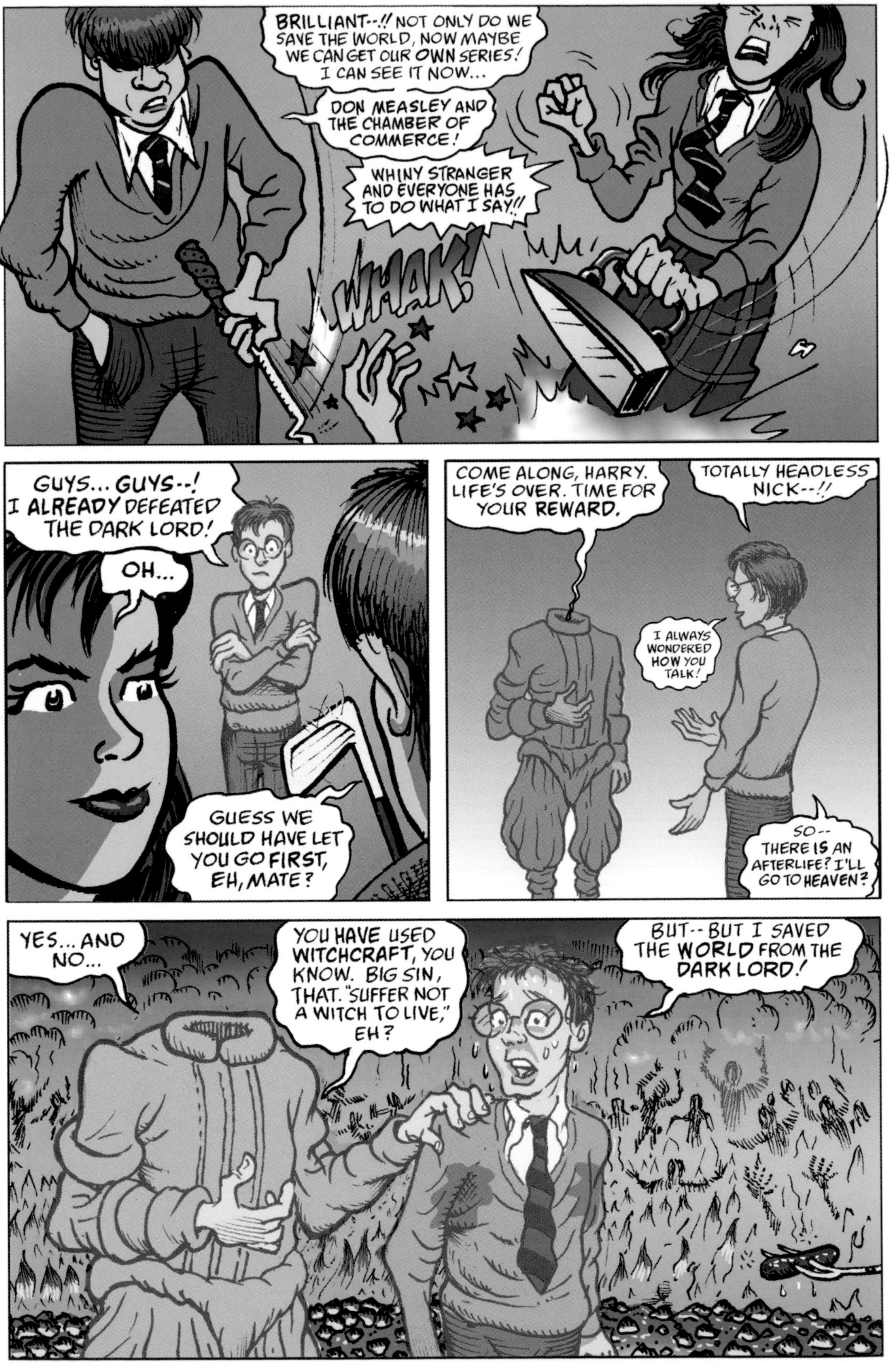
BRILLIANT--!! NOT ONLY DO WE SAVE THE WORLD, NOW MAYBE WE CAN GET OUR OWN SERIES! I CAN SEE IT NOW...
DON MEASLEY AND THE CHAMBER OF COMMERCE!
WHINY STRANGER AND EVERYONE HAS TO DO WHAT I SAY!!
WHAK!
GUYS... GUYS--! I ALREADY DEFEATED THE DARK LORD!
OH...
GUESS WE SHOULD HAVE LET YOU GO FIRST, EH, MATE?
COME ALONG, HARRY. LIFE'S OVER. TIME FOR YOUR REWARD.
TOTALLY HEADLESS NICK--!!
I ALWAYS WONDERED HOW YOU TALK!
SO-- THERE IS AN AFTERLIFE? I'LL GO TO HEAVEN?
YES... AND NO...
YOU HAVE USED WITCHCRAFT, YOU KNOW. BIG SIN, THAT. "SUFFER NOT A WITCH TO LIVE," EH?
BUT-- BUT I SAVED THE WORLD FROM THE DARK LORD!

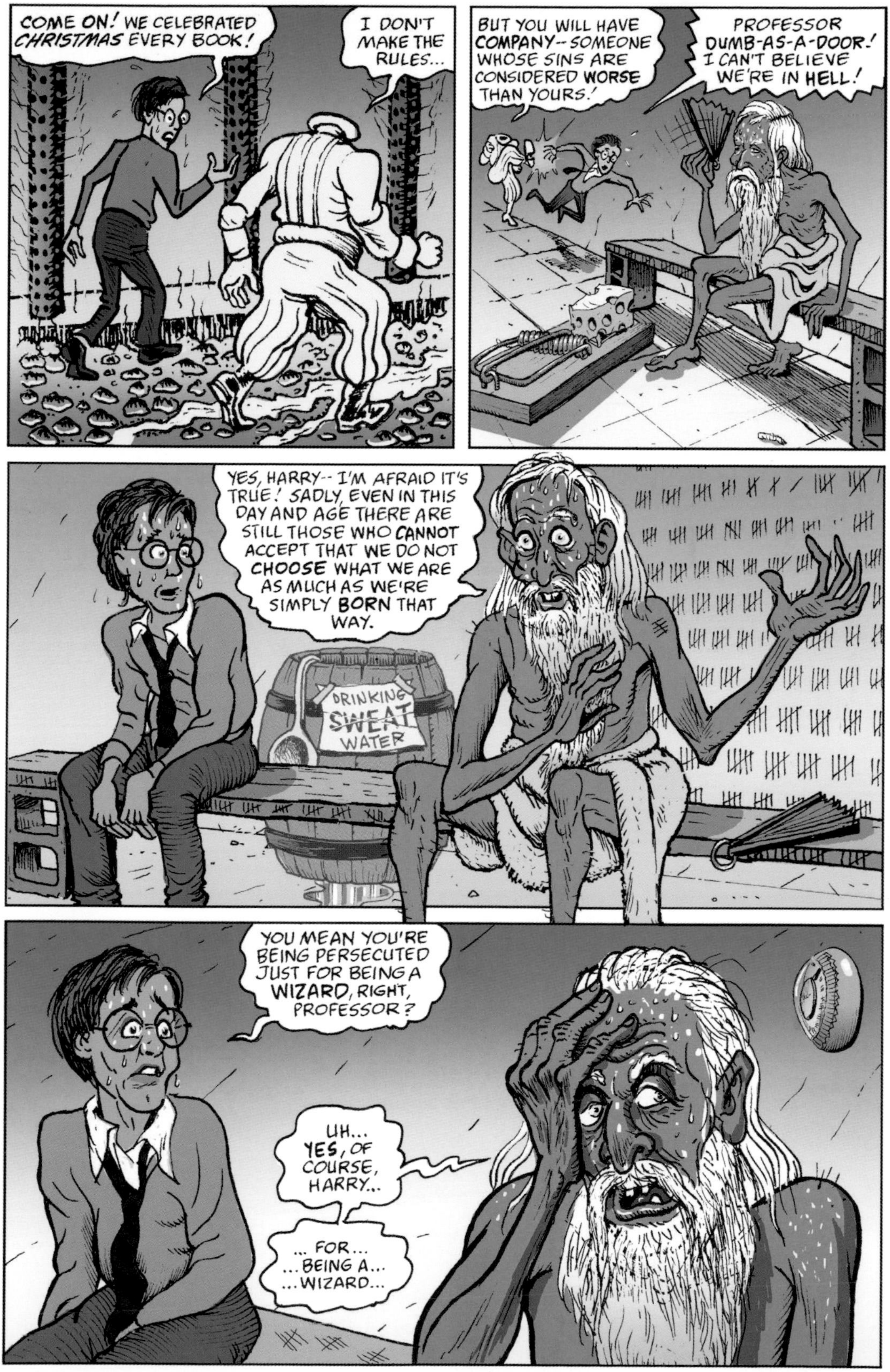

COME ON! WE CELEBRATED CHRISTMAS EVERY BOOK!
I DON'T MAKE THE RULES...
BUT YOU WILL HAVE COMPANY-- SOMEONE WHOSE SINS ARE CONSIDERED WORSE THAN YOURS!
PROFESSOR DUMB-AS-A-DOOR! I CAN'T BELIEVE WE'RE IN HELL!
YES, HARRY-- I'M AFRAID IT'S TRUE! SADLY, EVEN IN THIS DAY AND AGE THERE ARE STILL THOSE WHO CANNOT ACCEPT THAT WE DO NOT CHOOSE WHAT WE ARE AS MUCH AS WE'RE SIMPLY BORN THAT WAY.
DRINKING SWEAT WATER
YOU MEAN YOU'RE BEING PERSECUTED JUST FOR BEING A WIZARD, RIGHT, PROFESSOR?
UH... YES, OF COURSE, HARRY...
... FOR... ...BEING A... ...WIZARD...

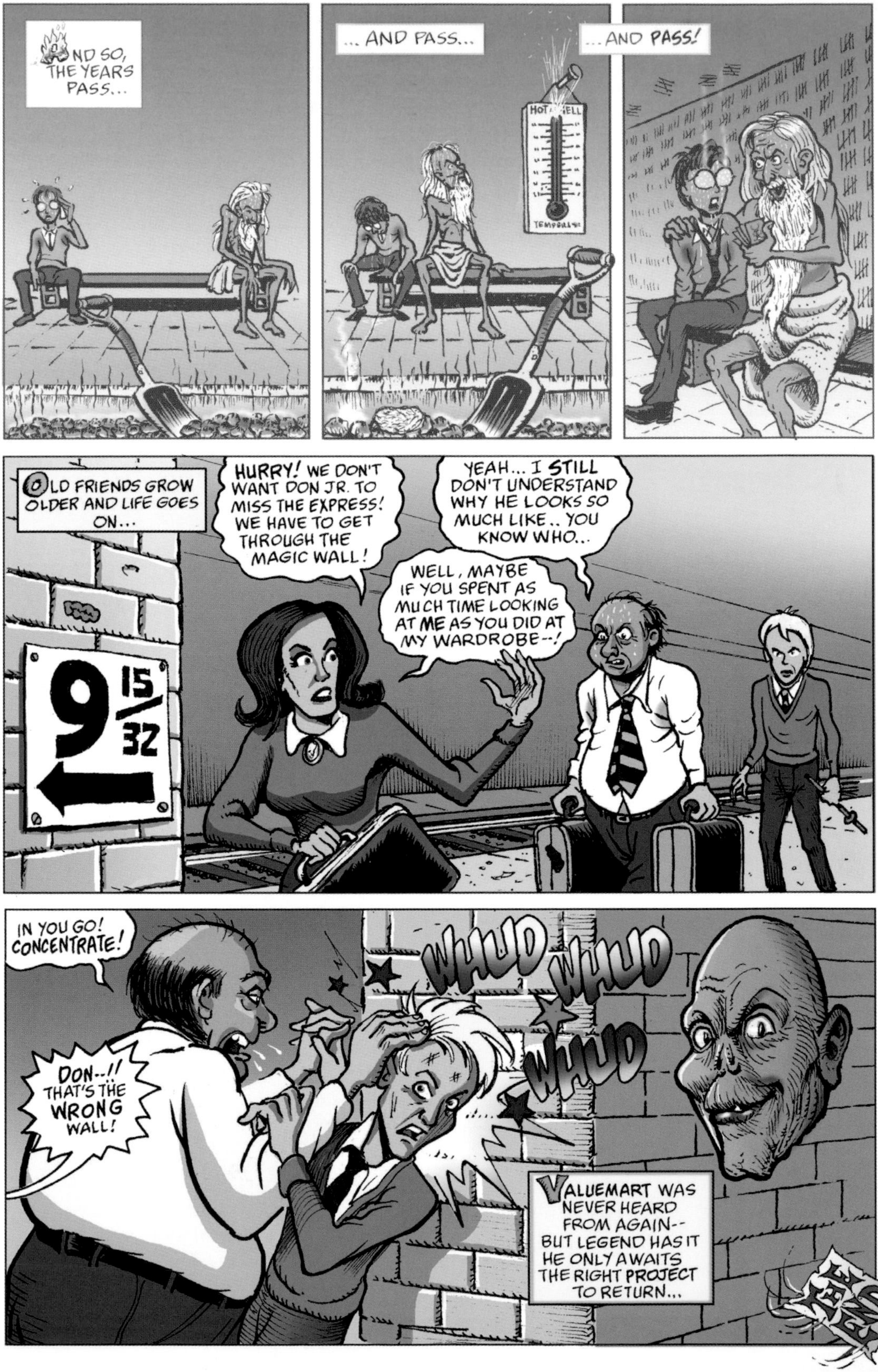
AND SO, THE YEARS PASS...
... AND PASS...
... AND PASS!
OLD FRIENDS GROW OLDER AND LIFE GOES ON...
HURRY! WE DON'T WANT DON JR. TO MISS THE EXPRESS! WE HAVE TO GET THROUGH THE MAGIC WALL!
YEAH... I STILL DON'T UNDERSTAND WHY HE LOOKS SO MUCH LIKE.. YOU KNOW WHO...
WELL, MAYBE IF YOU SPENT AS MUCH TIME LOOKING AT ME AS YOU DID AT MY WARDROBE--!
9 15/32
IN YOU GO! CONCENTRATE!
WHUD WHUD WHUD
DON--!! THAT'S THE WRONG WALL!
VALUEMART WAS NEVER HEARD FROM AGAIN-- BUT LEGEND HAS IT HE ONLY AWAITS THE RIGHT PROJECT TO RETURN...
THE END

# WATCH OUT FOR PAPERCUTZ™

Welcome to the pun-filled premiere of PAPERCUTZ SLICES, the new graphic novel series dedicated to cutting up your favorite pop culture icons! I'm Jim Salicrup, your potty-trained Editor-in-Chief, here to provide a little behind-the-scenes info on both Papercutz and PAPERCUTZ SLICES.

Papercutz, is the feisty, upstart graphic novel publisher which proudly brings you such incredible graphics novels such as BIONICLE, featuring all sorts of living robots with all sorts of funny names; CLASSICS ILLUSTRATED, the graphic novel series that takes great big novels and turns them into fast-paced comics (kinda like what's going on here in PAPERCUTZ SLICES, but not as funny); NANCY DREW, the sophisticated graphic novel series featuring America's favorite Girl Detective (and co-written by PAPERCUTZ SLICES's Stefan Petrucha), and TALES FROM THE CRYPT, the all-new graphic novel incarnation of the classic horror comic (with lots of contributions from Stefan as well as Rick Parker!). In other words, Papercutz is perhaps the most exciting, most-fun graphic novel publisher of all time, featuring comics by many of the greatest comics writers and artists ever. If you love comics, then you love Papercutz!

As for PAPERCUTZ SLICES, it's an all-new graphic novel series brought to you by writer Stefan Petrucha and artist Rick Parker. Stefan has been writing brilliant comics for years, featuring characters as diverse as Mickey Mouse, Spider-Man, Fox Mulder and Dana Skully, the Dana Girls (no relation), Duckman, Miracleman, and Lance Barnes, Post-Nuke Dick. He's also written equally brilliant novels such as *Making God*, *Teen Inc.*, *The Shadow of Frankenstein*, *The Rule of Won*, four volumes in the *Time Tripper* series, and more. Rick Parker has been drawing funny pictures since he was a little boy, and has drawn such insane comics as BEAVIS AND BUTT-HEAD and "Diary of a Stinky Dead Kid." In fact, it was on "Diary of a Stinky Dead Kid" that Stefan and Rick first worked together. Not only did that unauthorized parody in TALES FROM THE CRYPT #8 meet with critical acclaim, but it also became one of the biggest selling graphic novels from Papercutz.

It didn't take long before Stefan was suggesting that Papercutz should consider an ongoing graphic novel filled with same kind of pop culture parodies, and just like that PA-PERCUTZ SLICES was born (Hey! We're no dummies!) Stefan also insisted on starting off with "Harry Potty and the Deathly Boring," and again we think he was 100% correct! Let us know what you think—email me at salicrup@papercutz or send your snailmail to PAPERCUTZ SLICES, 40 Exchange Place, Suite 1308, New York, NY 10005. We may run the most interesting (or dumbest) comments in PAPERCUTZ SLICES #2.

In the meantime, check out the all-new follow-up to "Diary of a Stinky Dead Kid" in TALES FROM THE CRYPT 9 "Wickeder," on sale now. It's written by Stefan Petrucha (and daughter Margo Kinney-Petrucha) and drawn by Diego Jourdan, who drew the very first picture of Glugg, the Stinky Dead Kid for the cover of TALES FROM THE CRYPT #8. For a special sneak preview—just keep turning the pages, you'll find it soon enough!

So that's it for now. Be sure to come back for PAPERCUTZ SLICES #2 "Breaking Down"! If you can't figure out what we'll be spoofing based on the title, here's a big clue-- an actual quote from author Stephenie Meyer: "I'm burned out on vampires right now." So are we, but that just makes lampooning shiny vampires that much more fun!

Thanks,

*Jim*

# PRESENTING AN ALL-NEW SERIES FROM PAPERCUTZ...

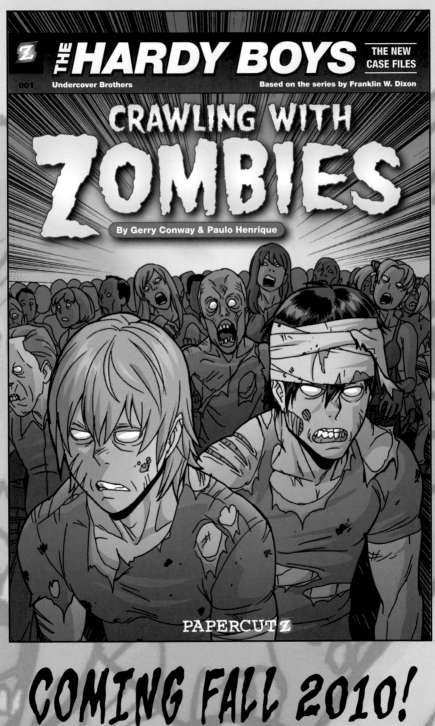

# COMING FALL 2010!

SPECIAL PREVIEW OF
TALES FROM THE CRYPT #9 "WICKEDER"—

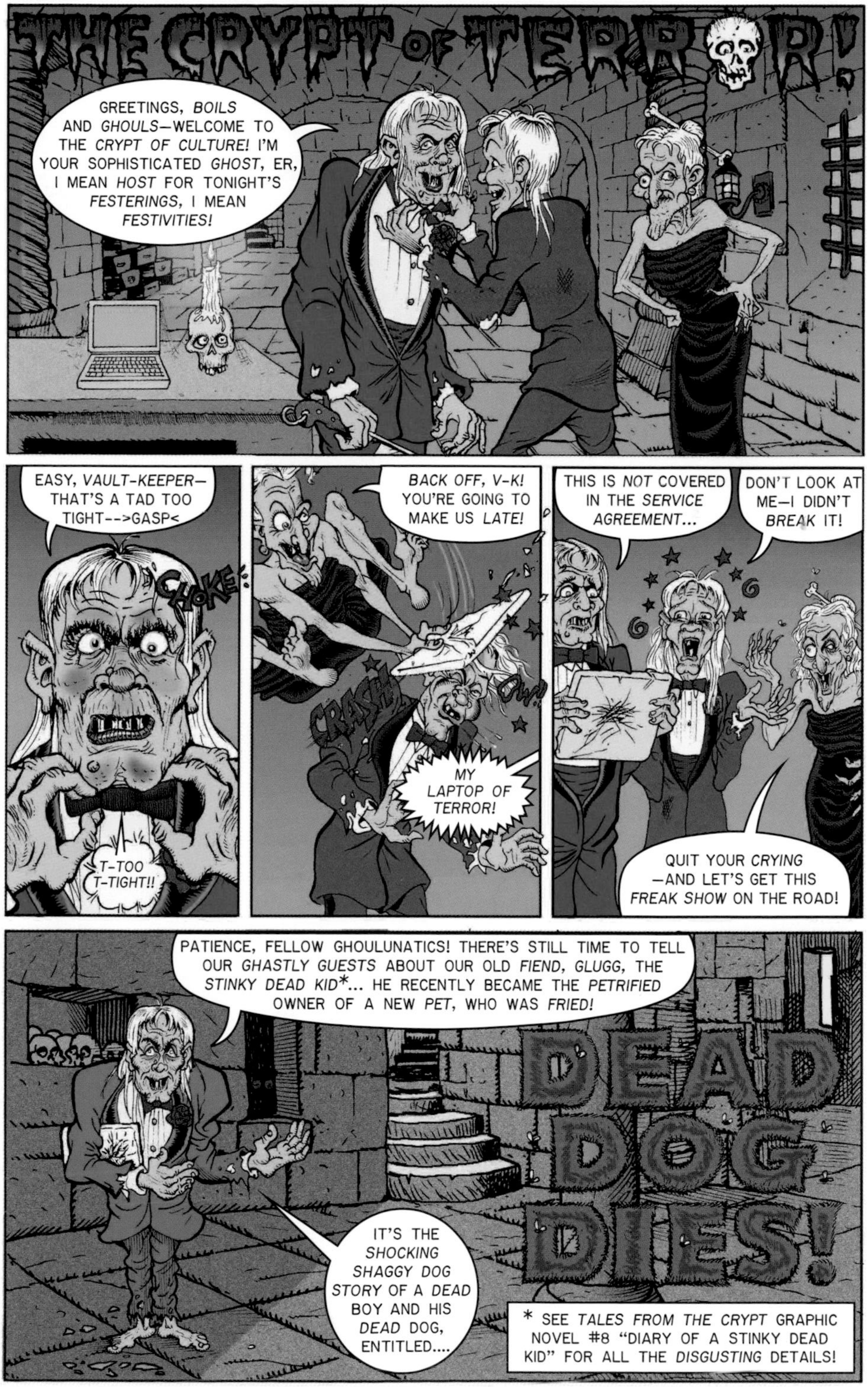
THE CRYPT OF TERROR!
GREETINGS, BOILS AND GHOULS—WELCOME TO THE CRYPT OF CULTURE! I'M YOUR SOPHISTICATED GHOST, ER, I MEAN HOST FOR TONIGHT'S FESTERINGS, I MEAN FESTIVITIES!
EASY, VAULT-KEEPER—THAT'S A TAD TOO TIGHT-->GASP<
CHOKE
T-TOO T-TIGHT!!
BACK OFF, V-K! YOU'RE GOING TO MAKE US LATE!
CRASH!
OW!!
MY LAPTOP OF TERROR!
THIS IS NOT COVERED IN THE SERVICE AGREEMENT...
DON'T LOOK AT ME—I DIDN'T BREAK IT!
QUIT YOUR CRYING —AND LET'S GET THIS FREAK SHOW ON THE ROAD!
PATIENCE, FELLOW GHOULUNATICS! THERE'S STILL TIME TO TELL OUR GHASTLY GUESTS ABOUT OUR OLD FIEND, GLUGG, THE STINKY DEAD KID*... HE RECENTLY BECAME THE PETRIFIED OWNER OF A NEW PET, WHO WAS FRIED!
IT'S THE SHOCKING SHAGGY DOG STORY OF A DEAD BOY AND HIS DEAD DOG, ENTITLED....
DEAD DOG DIES!
* SEE TALES FROM THE CRYPT GRAPHIC NOVEL #8 "DIARY OF A STINKY DEAD KID" FOR ALL THE DISGUSTING DETAILS!

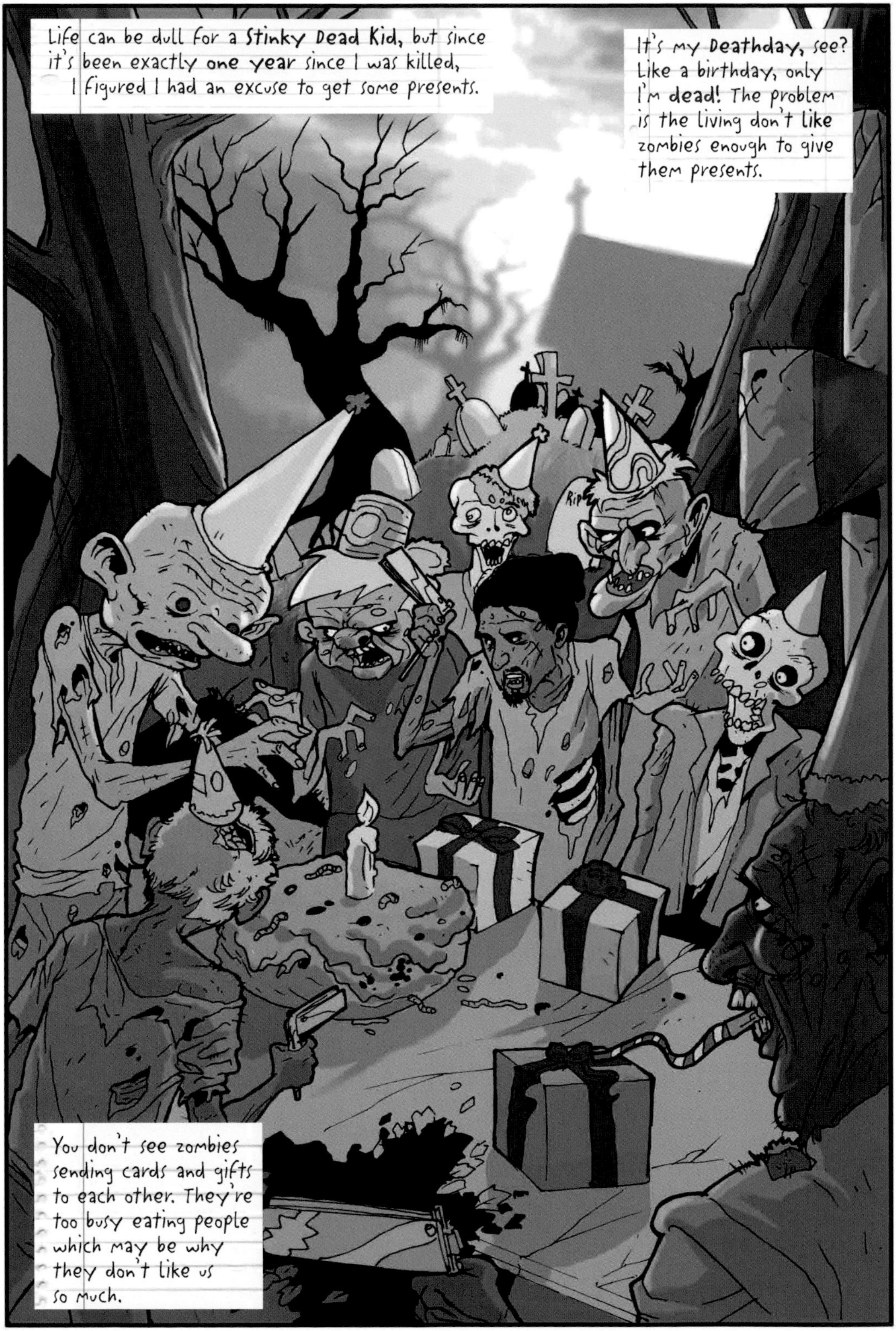
Life can be dull for a Stinky Dead Kid, but since it's been exactly one year since I was killed, I figured I had an excuse to get some presents.
It's my Deathday, see? Like a birthday, only I'm dead! The problem is the living don't like zombies enough to give them presents.
You don't see zombies sending cards and gifts to each other. They're too busy eating people which may be why they don't like us so much.

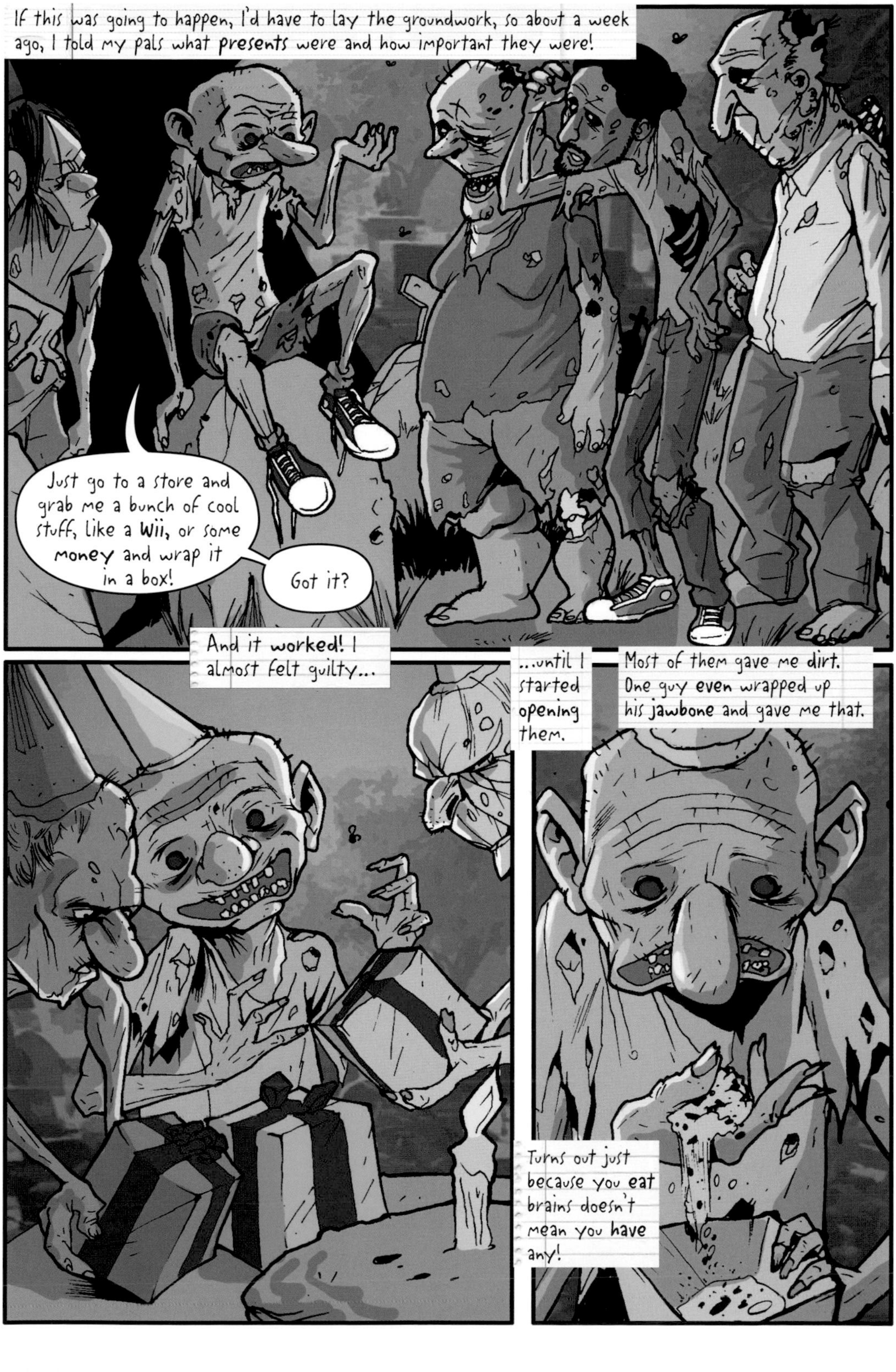

If this was going to happen, I'd have to lay the groundwork, so about a week ago, I told my pals what presents were and how important they were!
Just go to a store and grab me a bunch of cool stuff, like a Wii, or some money and wrap it in a box!
Got it?
And it worked! I almost felt guilty...
...until I started opening them.
Most of them gave me dirt. One guy even wrapped up his jawbone and gave me that.
Turns out just because you eat brains doesn't mean you have any!

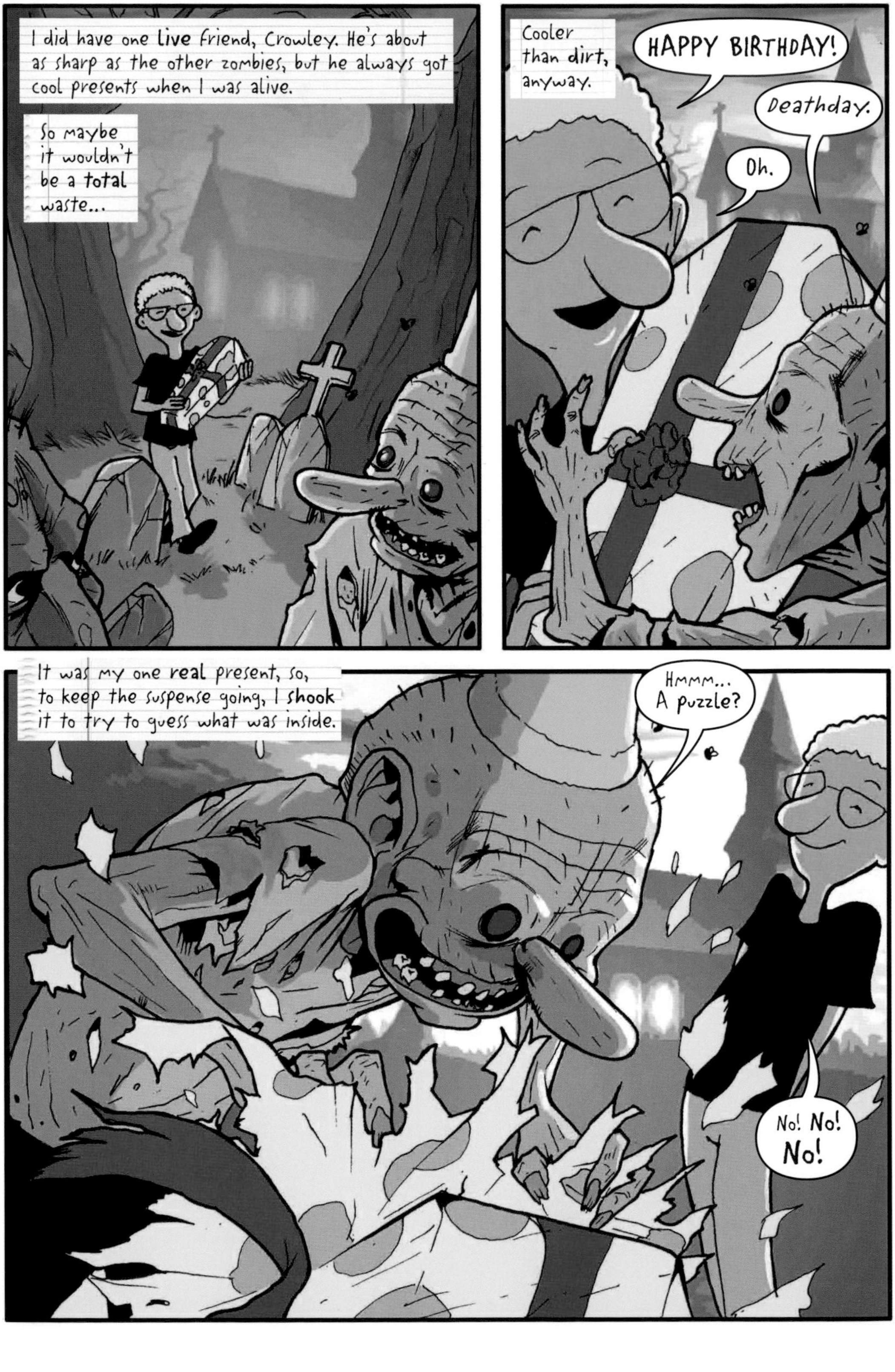
I did have one live friend, Crowley. He's about as sharp as the other zombies, but he always got cool presents when I was alive.
So maybe it wouldn't be a total waste...
Cooler than dirt, anyway.
HAPPY BIRTHDAY!
Deathday.
Oh.
It was my one real present, so, to keep the suspense going, I shook it to try to guess what was inside.
Hmmm... A puzzle?
No! No! No!

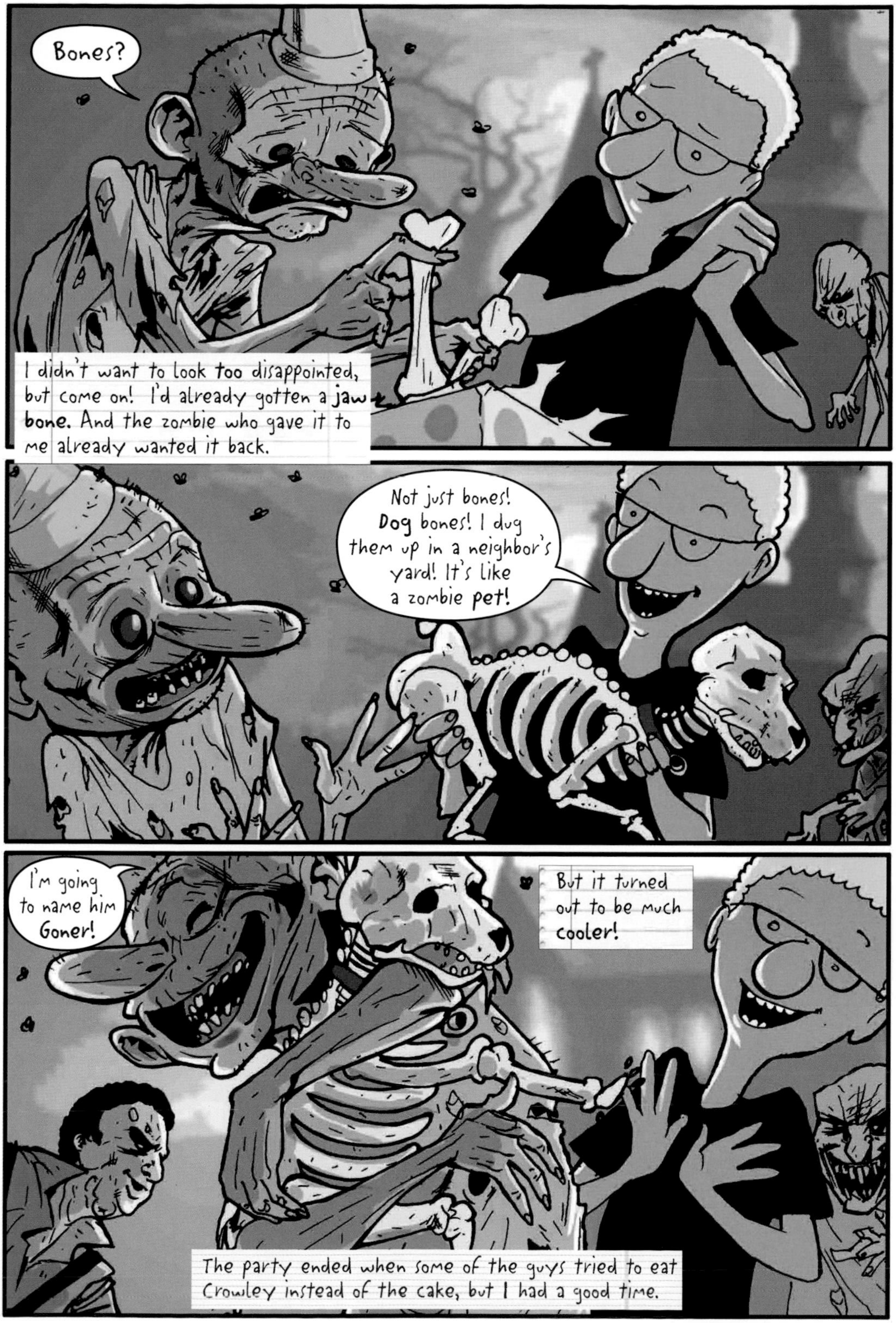
Bones?
I didn't want to look too disappointed, but come on! I'd already gotten a jaw bone. And the zombie who gave it to me already wanted it back.
Not just bones! Dog bones! I dug them up in a neighbor's yard! It's like a zombie pet!
I'm going to name him Goner!
But it turned out to be much cooler!
The party ended when some of the guys tried to eat Crowley instead of the cake, but I had a good time.

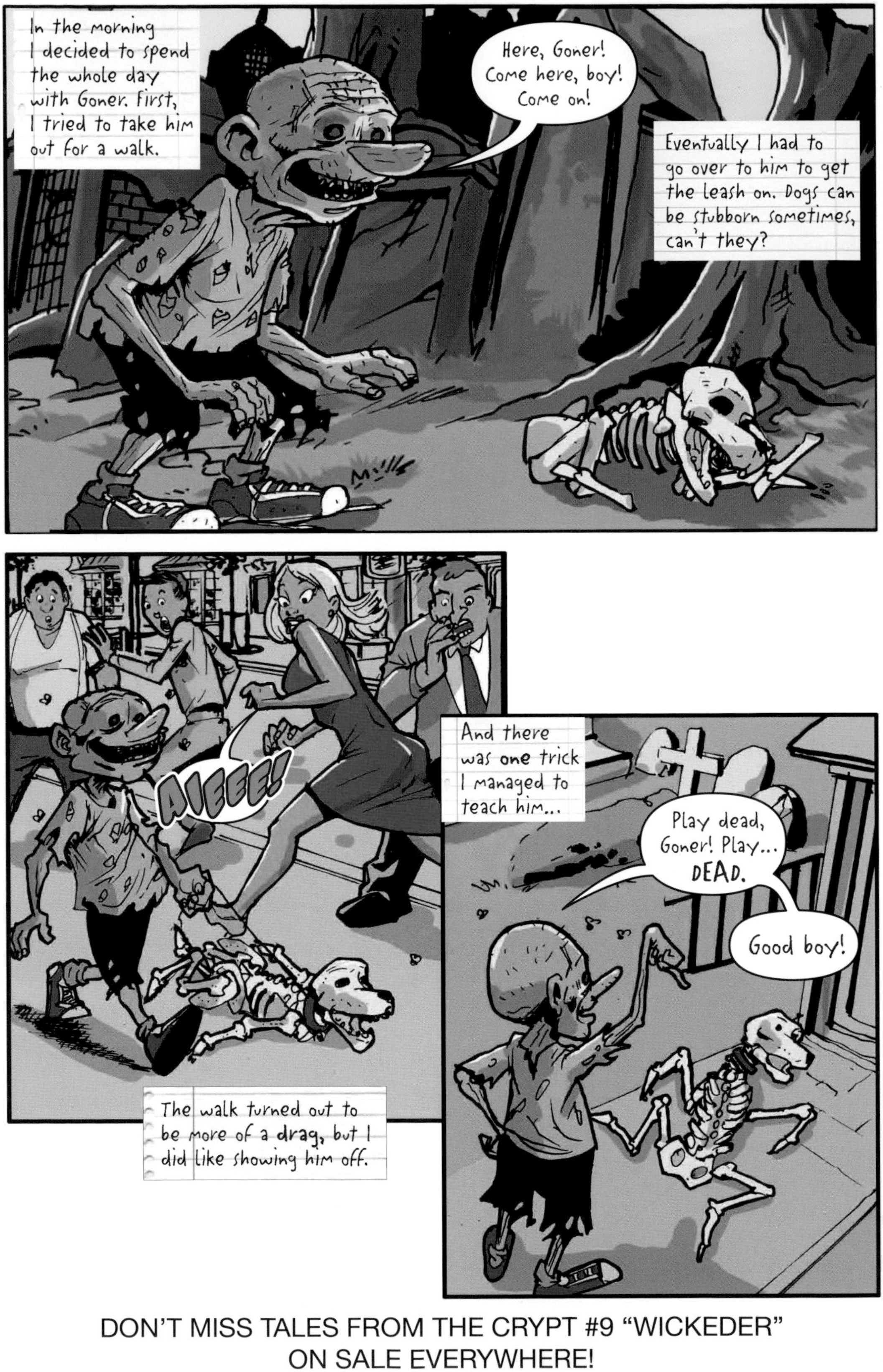
In the morning I decided to spend the whole day with Goner. First, I tried to take him out for a walk.
Here, Goner! Come here, boy! Come on!
Eventually I had to go over to him to get the leash on. Dogs can be stubborn sometimes, can't they?
AIEEE!
The walk turned out to be more of a drag, but I did like showing him off.
And there was one trick I managed to teach him...
Play dead, Goner! Play... DEAD.
Good boy!

DON'T MISS TALES FROM THE CRYPT #9 "WICKEDER" ON SALE EVERYWHERE!